921
EAR

Burleigh, Robert.

Amelia Earhart free
in the skies.

34880030034693

$14.40

DATE			

BAKER & TAYLOR

AMELIA EARHART

FREE IN THE SKIES

ROBERT BURLEIGH

ILLUSTRATED BY BILL WYLIE

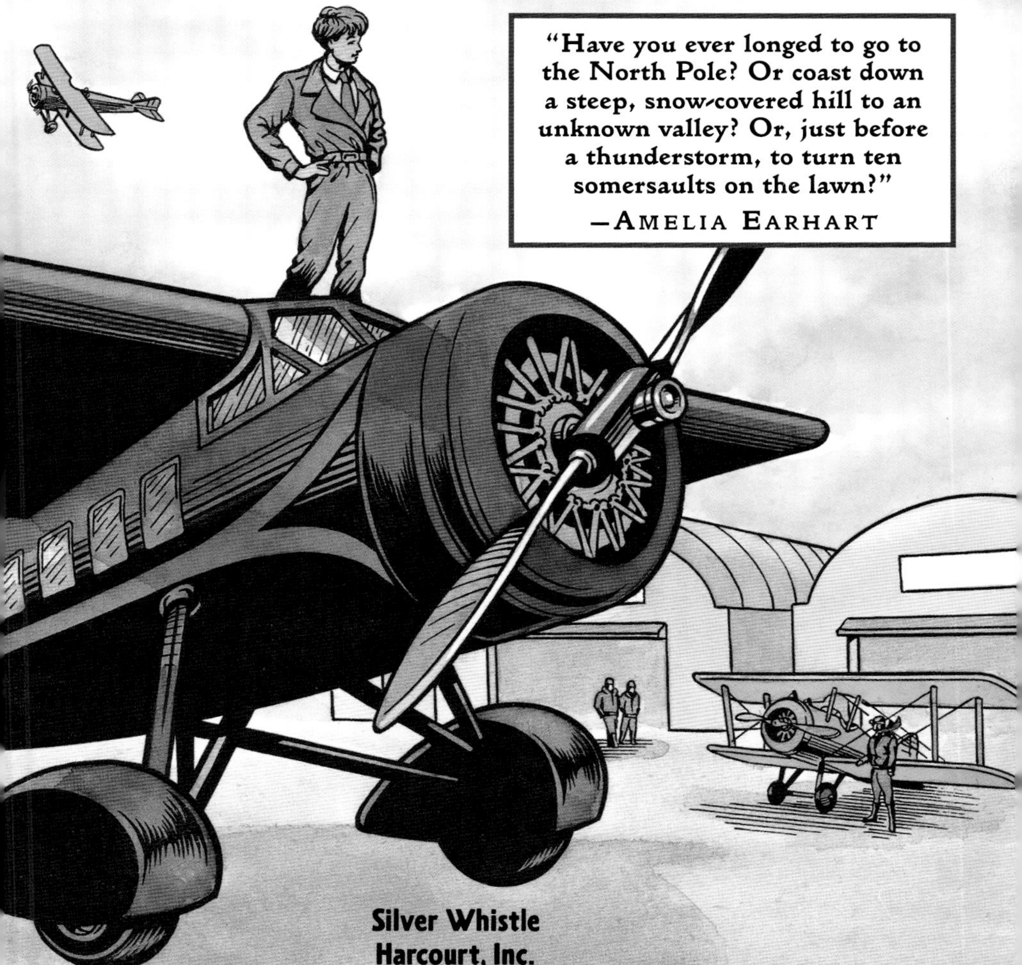

"Have you ever longed to go to the North Pole? Or coast down a steep, snow-covered hill to an unknown valley? Or, just before a thunderstorm, to turn ten somersaults on the lawn?"

—AMELIA EARHART

Silver Whistle
Harcourt, Inc.
Orlando Austin New York San Diego Toronto London

For Kate Myers Purdum
(and Dee Dee and Todd, too)
—R. B.

To Yuko, with love
—B. W.

Text copyright © 2003 by Robert Burleigh
Illustrations copyright © 2003 by Bill Wylie

Library of Congress Cataloging-in-Publication Data
Burleigh, Robert.
Amelia Earhart free in the skies/by Robert Burleigh; illustrated by Bill Wylie.
p. cm.
"Silver Whistle."
Summary: An illustrated biography of the world-famous woman pilot
known for her long and daring flights.
1. Earhart, Amelia, 1897–1937—Juvenile literature.   2. Air pilots—United States—Biography—
Juvenile literature.   3. Women air pilots—United States—Biography—Juvenile literature.
[1. Earhart, Amelia, 1897–1937.   2. Air pilots.   3. Women—Biography.]
1. Wylie, Bill, ill.   II. Title.   III. Series.
TL540.E3B873   2003
629. 13'092—dc21   2002000211
ISBN 0-15-202498-0
ISBN 0-15-216810-9 (pb)

First edition
A C E G H F D B
A C E G H F D B (pb)

Manufactured in China

The illustrations in this book were done in Luma dyes on Smooth watercolor paper.
The display type and speech balloons were created by Ken Lopez.
The text type was set in WhizBang.
Color separations by Bright Arts Ltd., Hong Kong
Manufactured by South China Printing Company, Ltd., China
This book was printed on totally chlorine-free
Enso Stora Matte paper.
Production supervision by
Sandra Grebenar and Ginger Boyer
Designed by Lydia D'moch

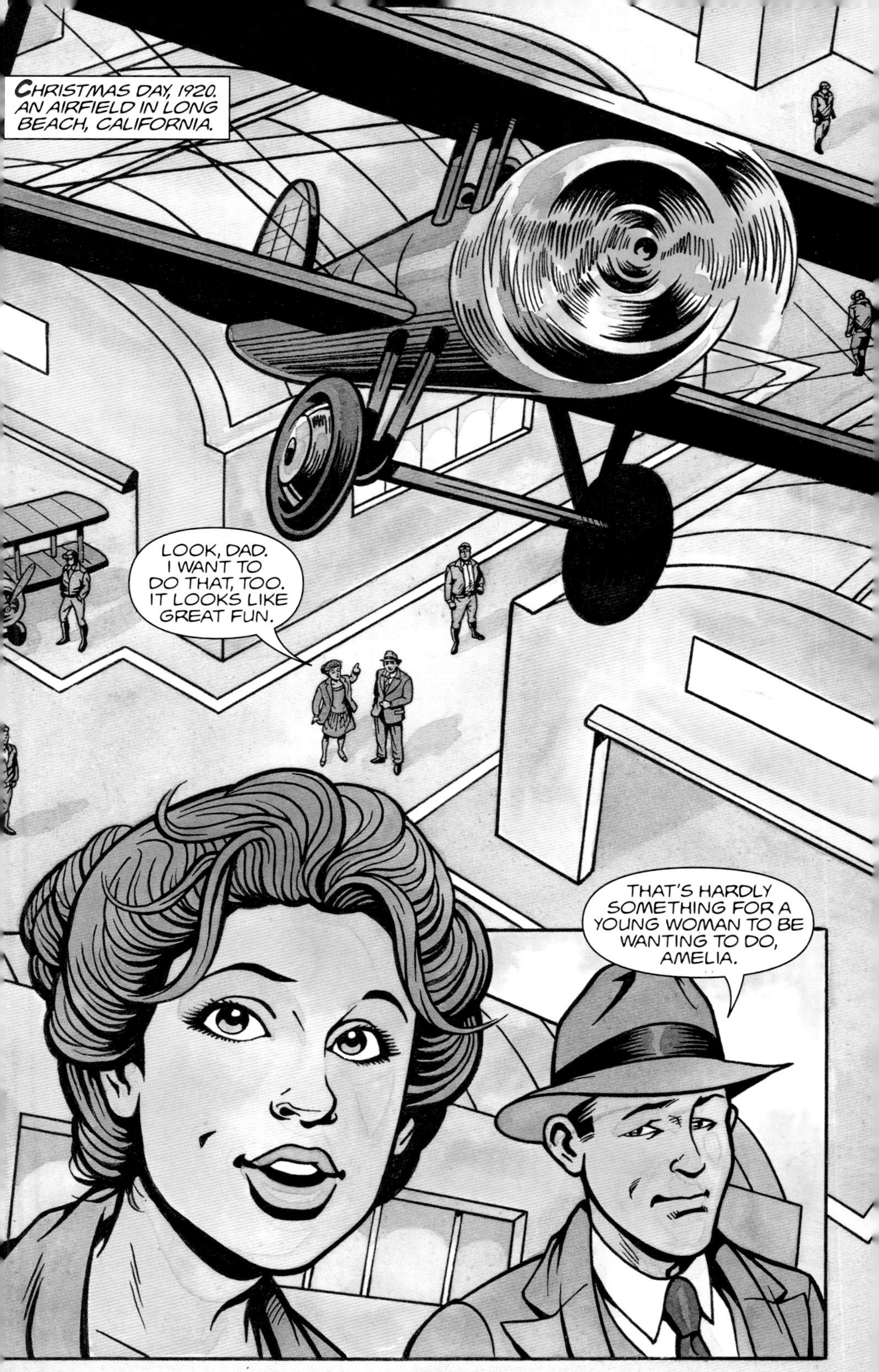
CHRISTMAS DAY, 1920. AN AIRFIELD IN LONG BEACH, CALIFORNIA.
LOOK, DAD. I WANT TO DO THAT, TOO. IT LOOKS LIKE GREAT FUN.
THAT'S HARDLY SOMETHING FOR A YOUNG WOMAN TO BE WANTING TO DO, AMELIA.

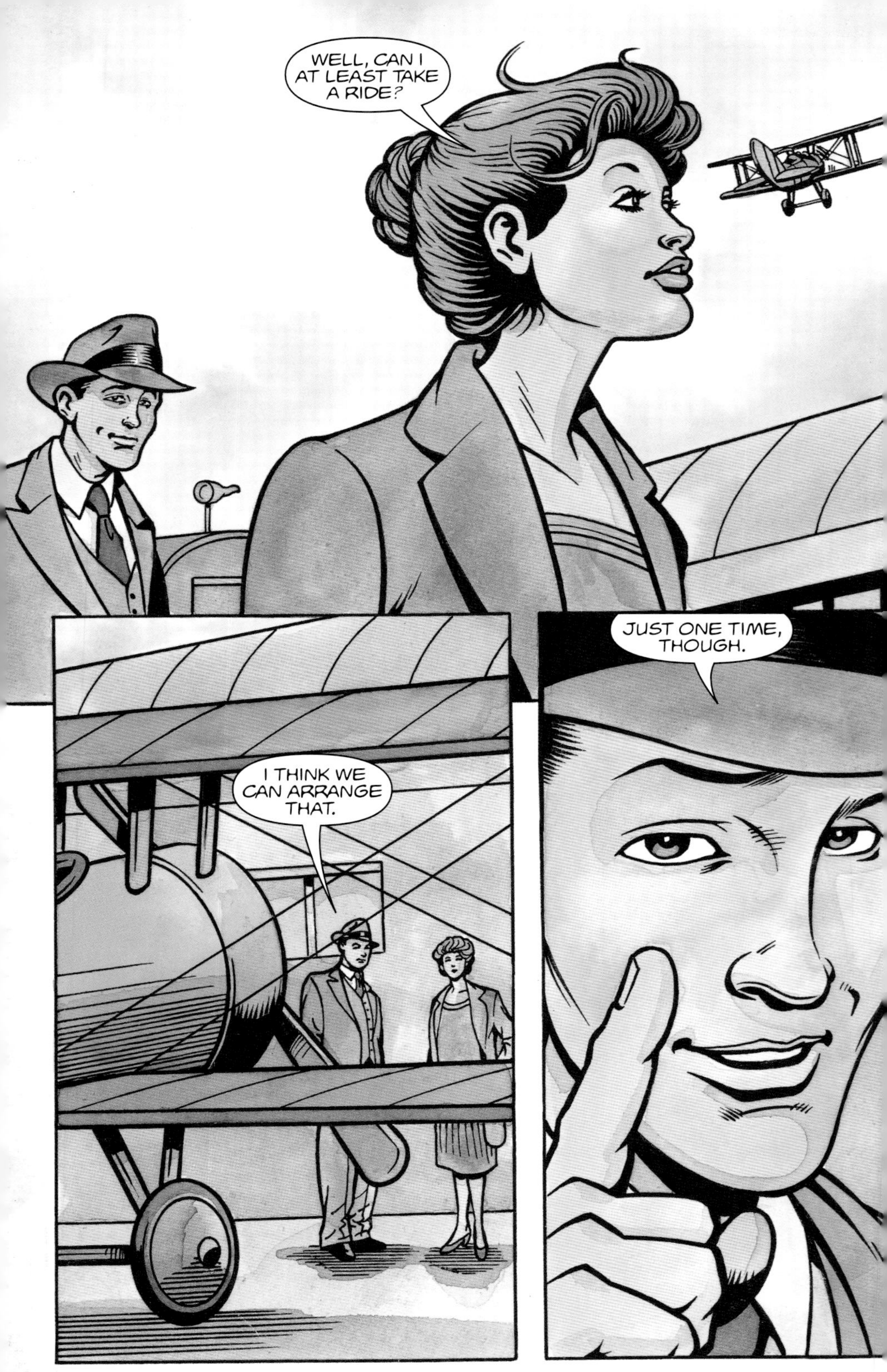
WELL, CAN I AT LEAST TAKE A RIDE?
I THINK WE CAN ARRANGE THAT.
JUST ONE TIME, THOUGH.

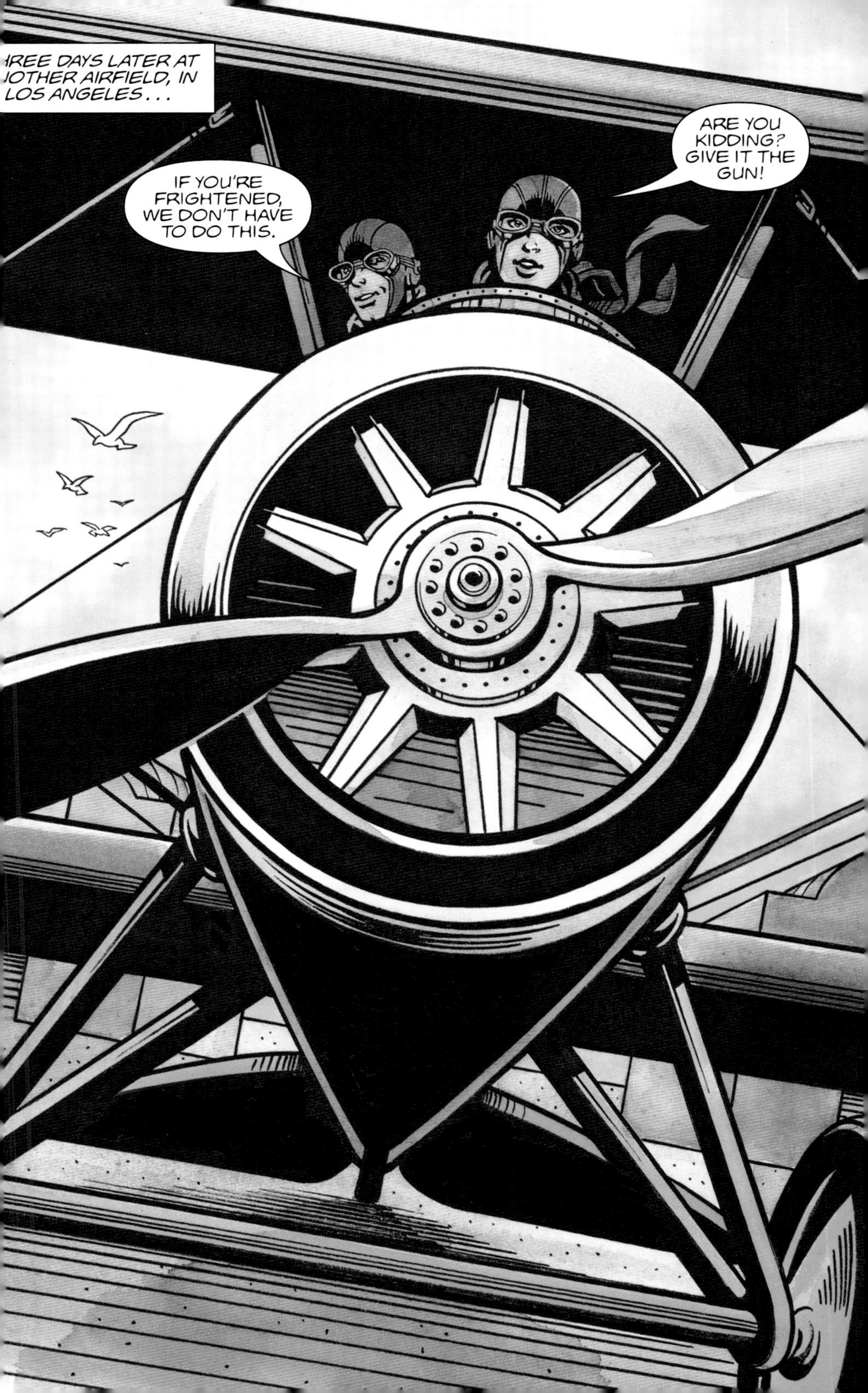
IREE DAYS LATER AT
IOTHER AIRFIELD, IN
LOS ANGELES...
IF YOU'RE FRIGHTENED, WE DON'T HAVE TO DO THIS.
ARE YOU KIDDING? GIVE IT THE GUN!

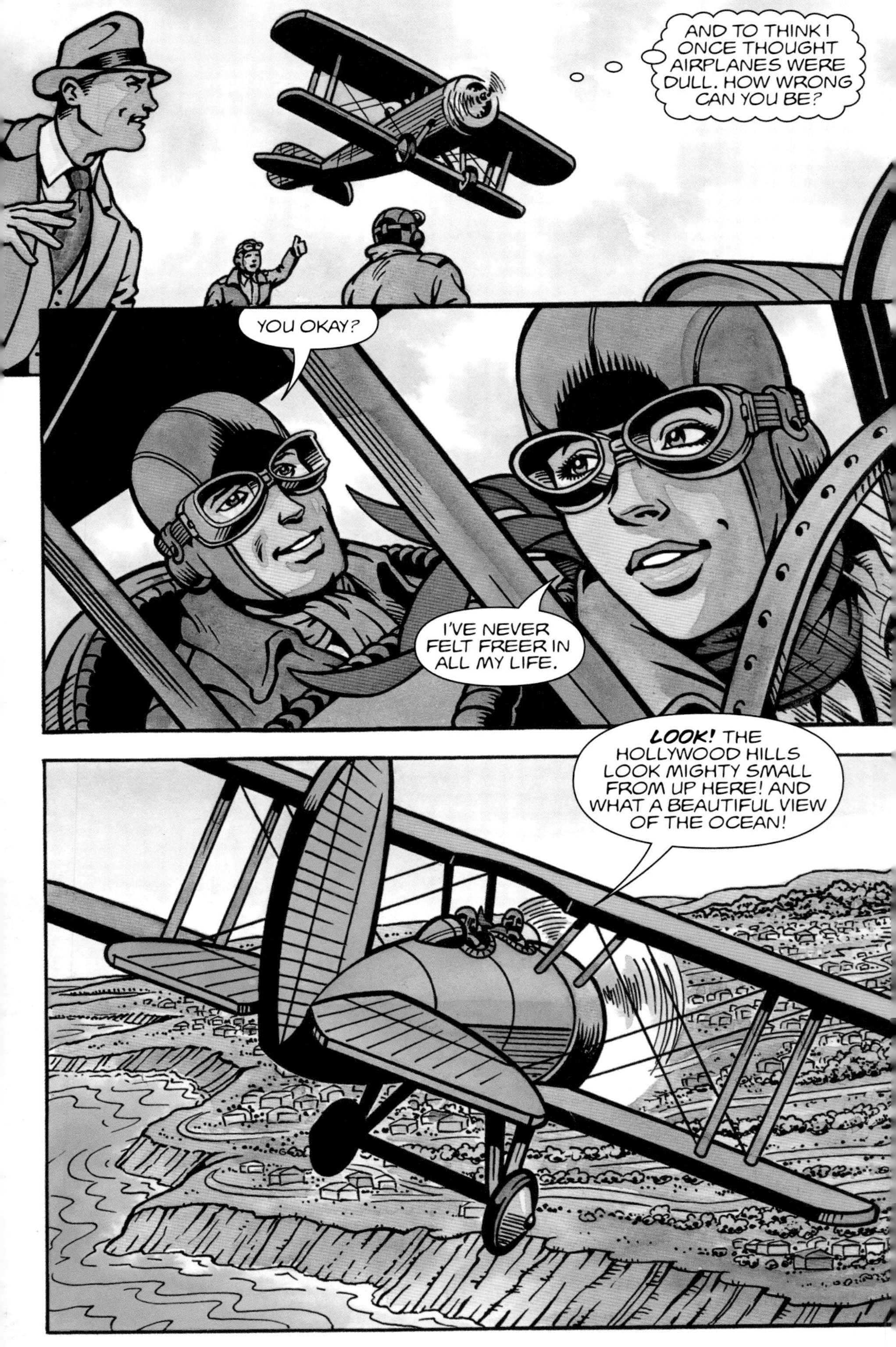
AND TO THINK I ONCE THOUGHT AIRPLANES WERE DULL. HOW WRONG CAN YOU BE?
YOU OKAY?
I'VE NEVER FELT FREER IN ALL MY LIFE.
LOOK! THE HOLLYWOOD HILLS LOOK MIGHTY SMALL FROM UP HERE! AND WHAT A BEAUTIFUL VIEW OF THE OCEAN!

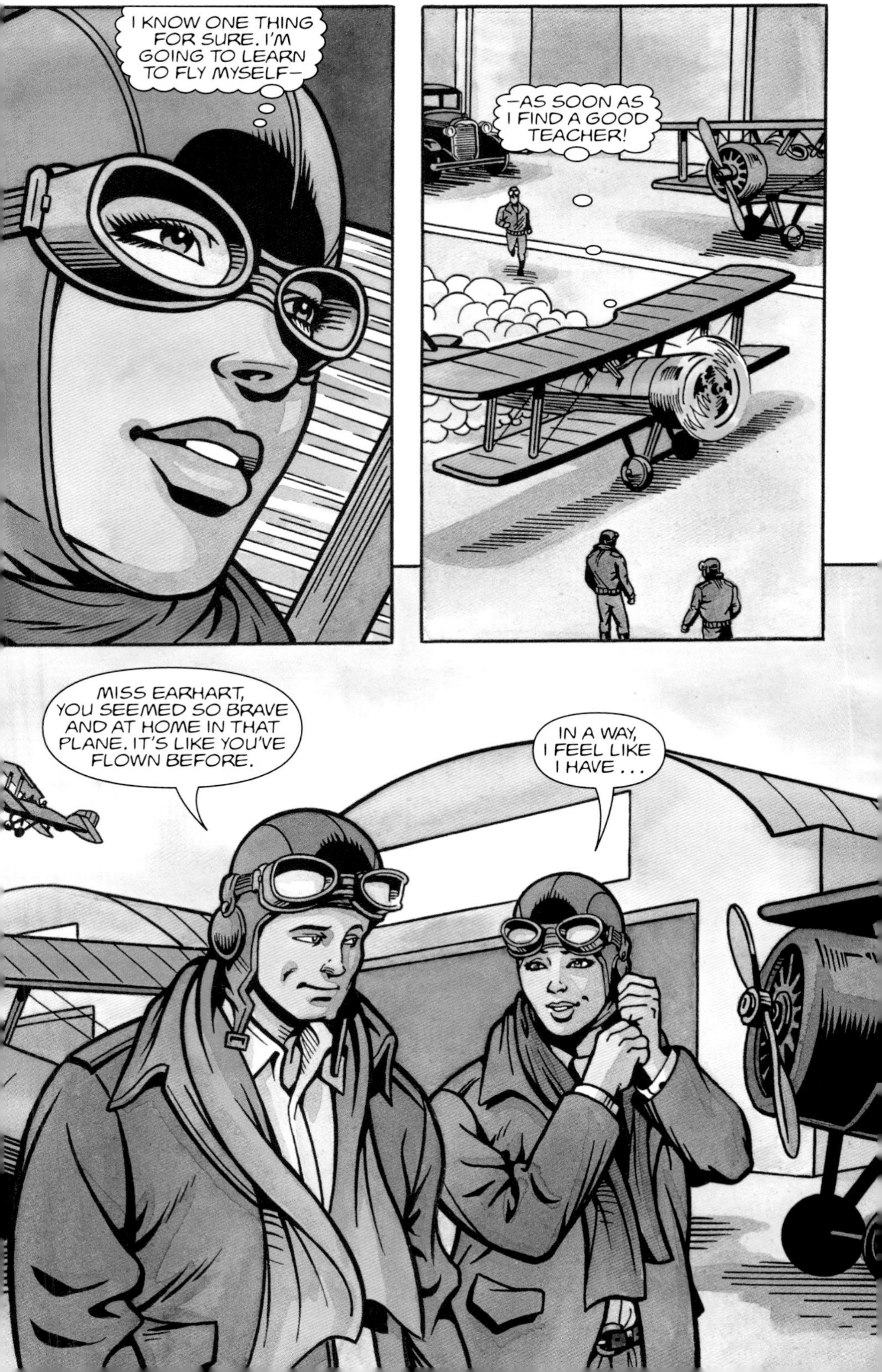
I KNOW ONE THING FOR SURE. I'M GOING TO LEARN TO FLY MYSELF—
—AS SOON AS I FIND A GOOD TEACHER!
MISS EARHART, YOU SEEMED SO BRAVE AND AT HOME IN THAT PLANE. IT'S LIKE YOU'VE FLOWN BEFORE.
IN A WAY, I FEEL LIKE I HAVE . . .

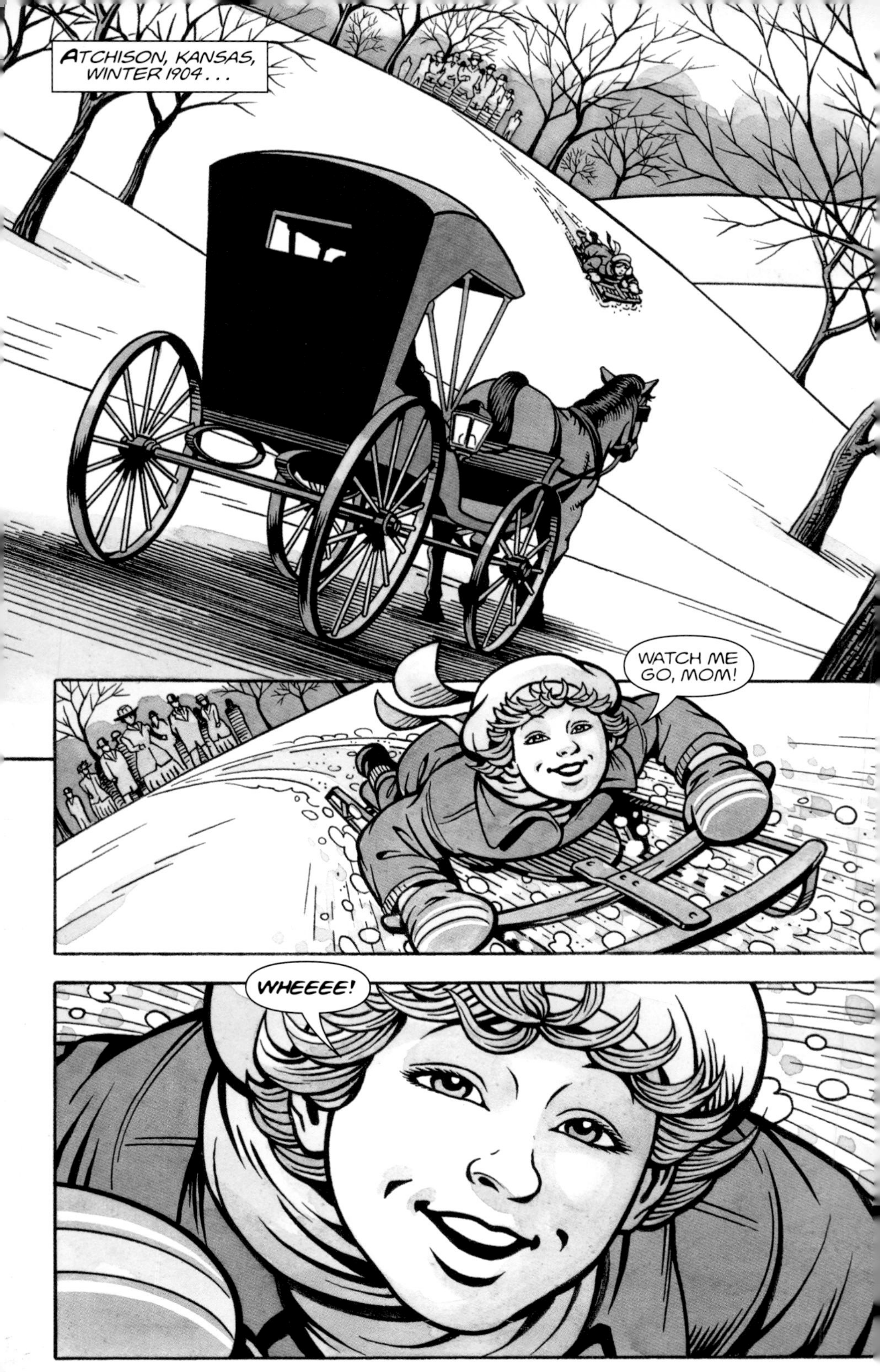
ATCHISON, KANSAS, WINTER 1904 . . .
WATCH ME GO, MOM!
WHEEEEE!

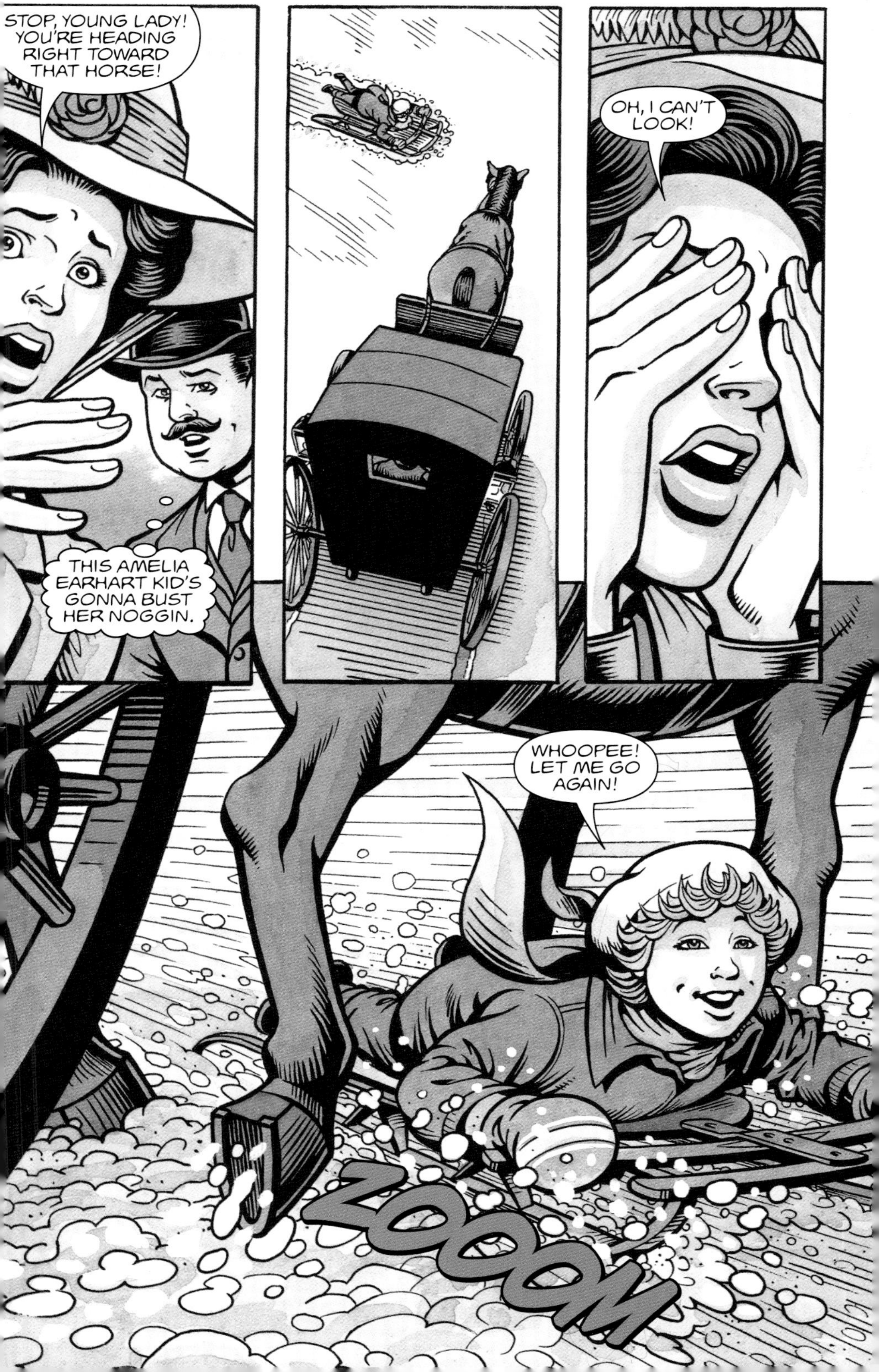
STOP, YOUNG LADY! YOU'RE HEADING RIGHT TOWARD THAT HORSE!
THIS AMELIA EARHART KID'S GONNA BUST HER NOGGIN.
OH, I CAN'T LOOK!
WHOOPEE! LET ME GO AGAIN!
ZOOOM

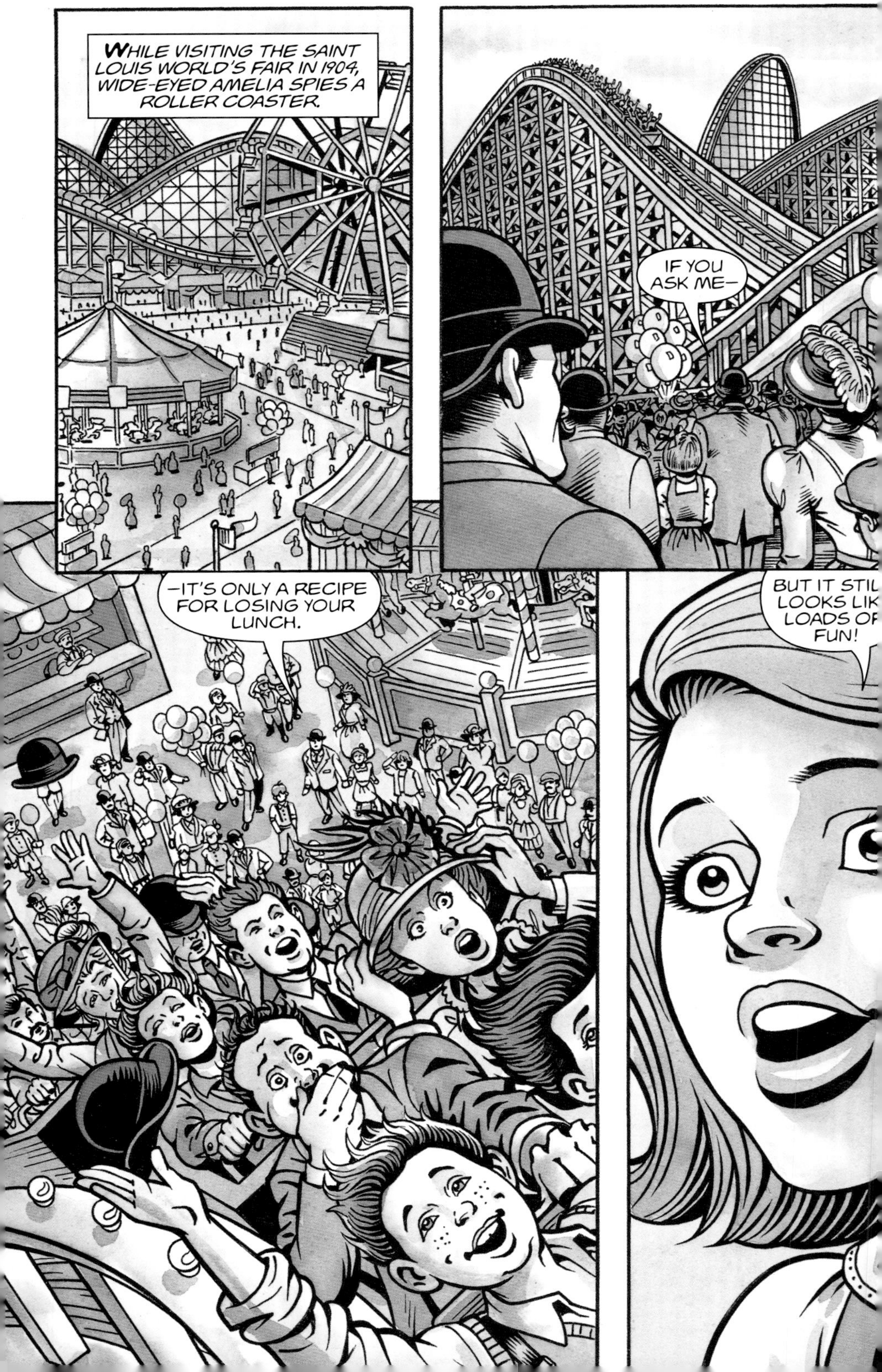
WHILE VISITING THE SAINT LOUIS WORLD'S FAIR IN 1904, WIDE-EYED AMELIA SPIES A ROLLER COASTER.
IF YOU ASK ME–
–IT'S ONLY A RECIPE FOR LOSING YOUR LUNCH.
BUT IT STIL LOOKS LIK LOADS OF FUN!

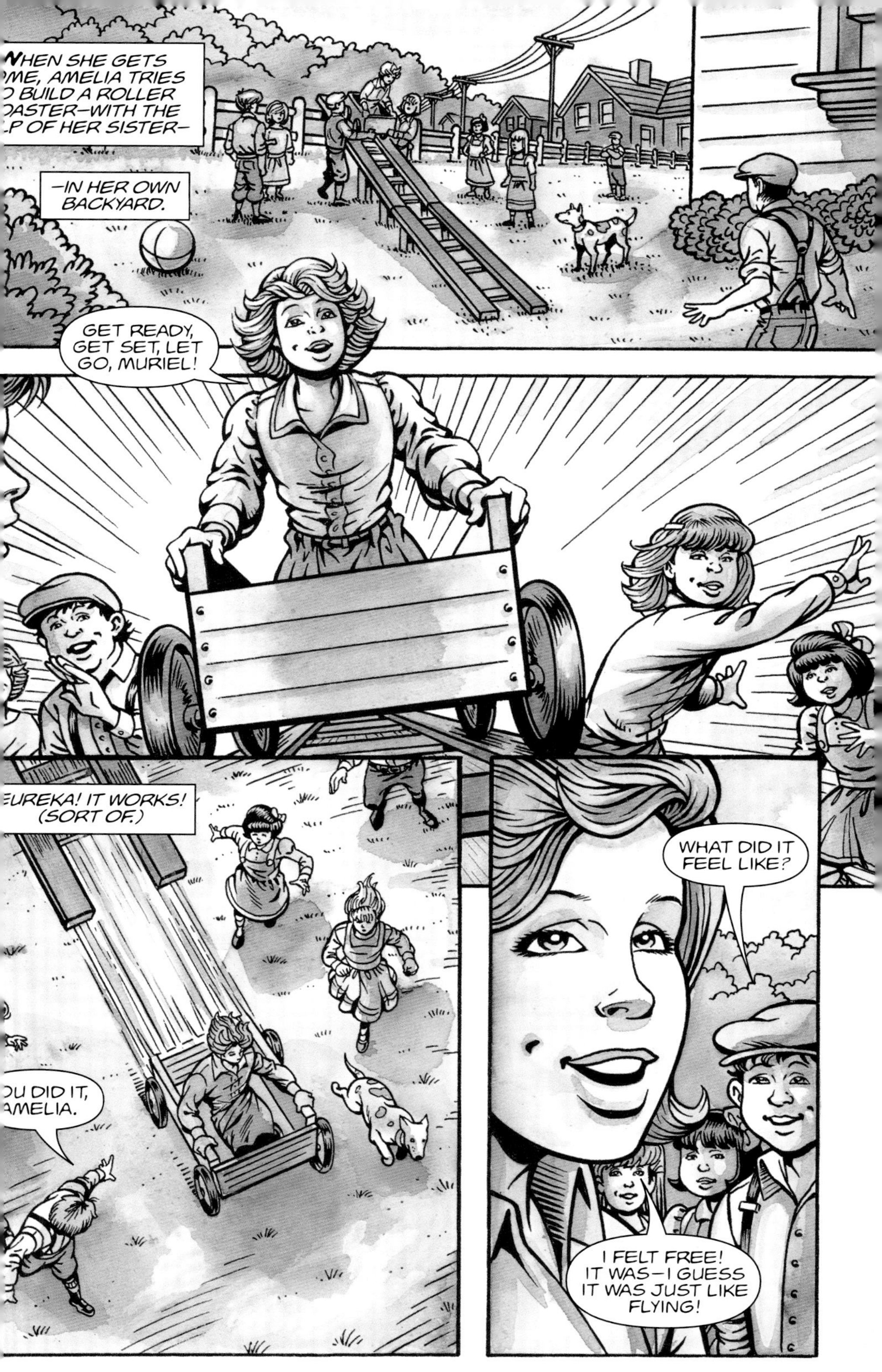

WHEN SHE GETS
OME, AMELIA TRIES
O BUILD A ROLLER
OASTER—WITH THE
LP OF HER SISTER—
—IN HER OWN
BACKYARD.
GET READY,
GET SET, LET
GO, MURIEL!
EUREKA! IT WORKS!
(SORT OF.)
OU DID IT,
AMELIA.
WHAT DID IT
FEEL LIKE?
I FELT FREE!
IT WAS—I GUESS
IT WAS JUST LIKE
FLYING!

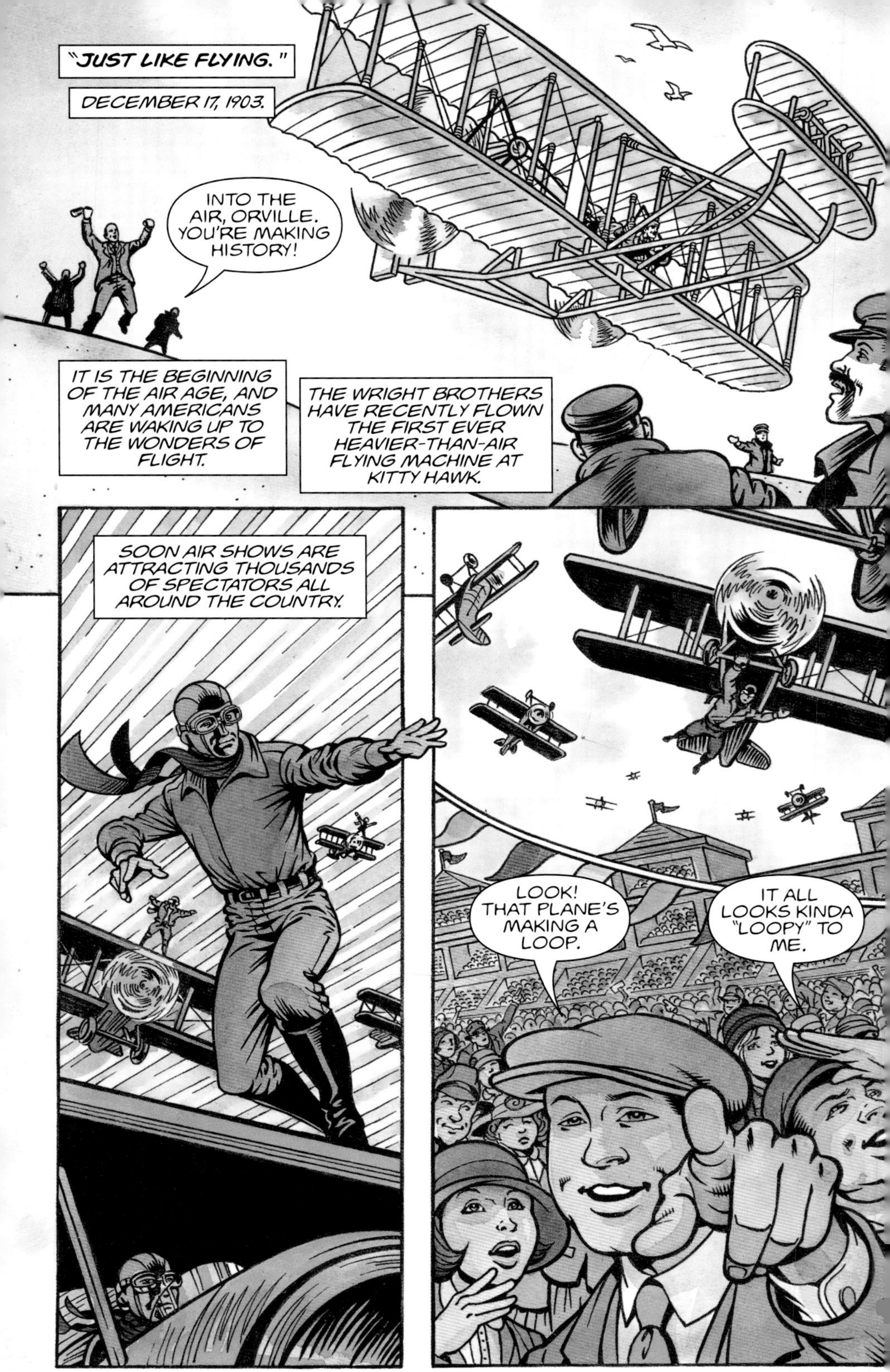
"JUST LIKE FLYING."
DECEMBER 17, 1903.
INTO THE AIR, ORVILLE. YOU'RE MAKING HISTORY!
IT IS THE BEGINNING OF THE AIR AGE, AND MANY AMERICANS ARE WAKING UP TO THE WONDERS OF FLIGHT.
THE WRIGHT BROTHERS HAVE RECENTLY FLOWN THE FIRST EVER HEAVIER-THAN-AIR FLYING MACHINE AT KITTY HAWK.
SOON AIR SHOWS ARE ATTRACTING THOUSANDS OF SPECTATORS ALL AROUND THE COUNTRY.
LOOK! THAT PLANE'S MAKING A LOOP.
IT ALL LOOKS KINDA "LOOPY" TO ME.

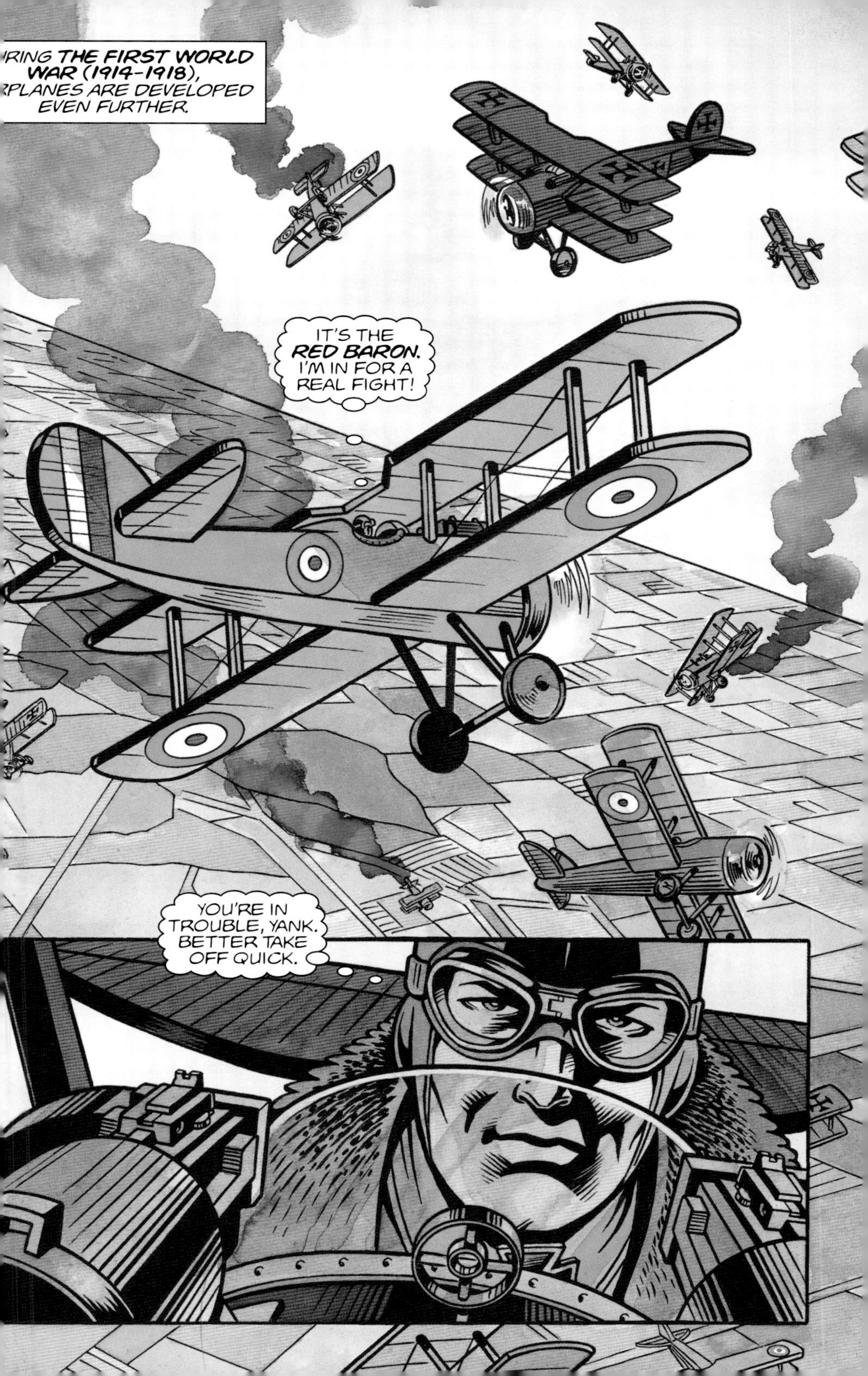
RING THE FIRST WORLD WAR (1914-1918), RPLANES ARE DEVELOPED EVEN FURTHER.
IT'S THE RED BARON. I'M IN FOR A REAL FIGHT!
YOU'RE IN TROUBLE, YANK. BETTER TAKE OFF QUICK.

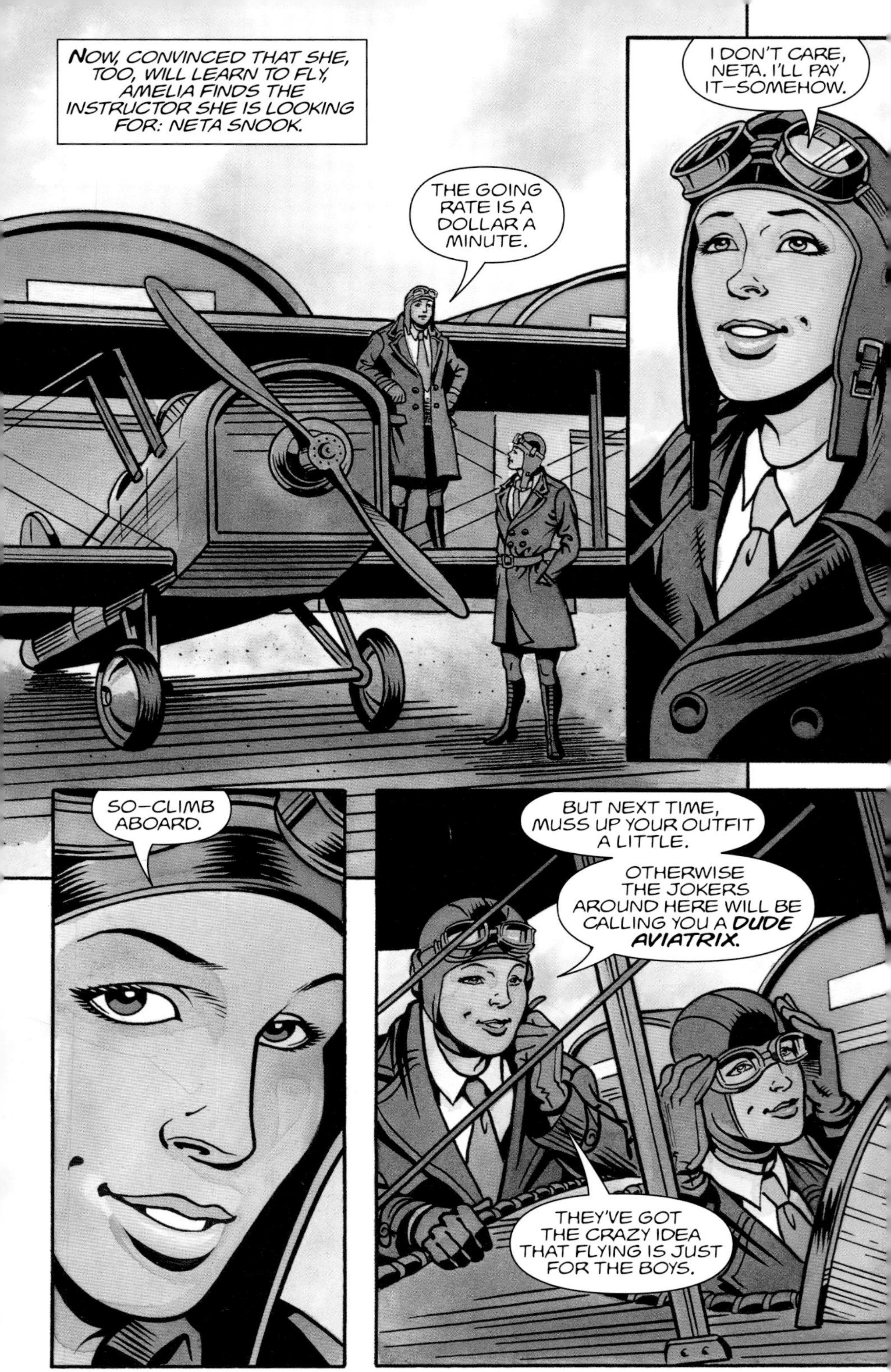
NOW, CONVINCED THAT SHE, TOO, WILL LEARN TO FLY, AMELIA FINDS THE INSTRUCTOR SHE IS LOOKING FOR: NETA SNOOK.
THE GOING RATE IS A DOLLAR A MINUTE.
I DON'T CARE, NETA. I'LL PAY IT—SOMEHOW.
SO—CLIMB ABOARD.
BUT NEXT TIME, MUSS UP YOUR OUTFIT A LITTLE.
OTHERWISE THE JOKERS AROUND HERE WILL BE CALLING YOU A DUDE AVIATRIX.
THEY'VE GOT THE CRAZY IDEA THAT FLYING IS JUST FOR THE BOYS.

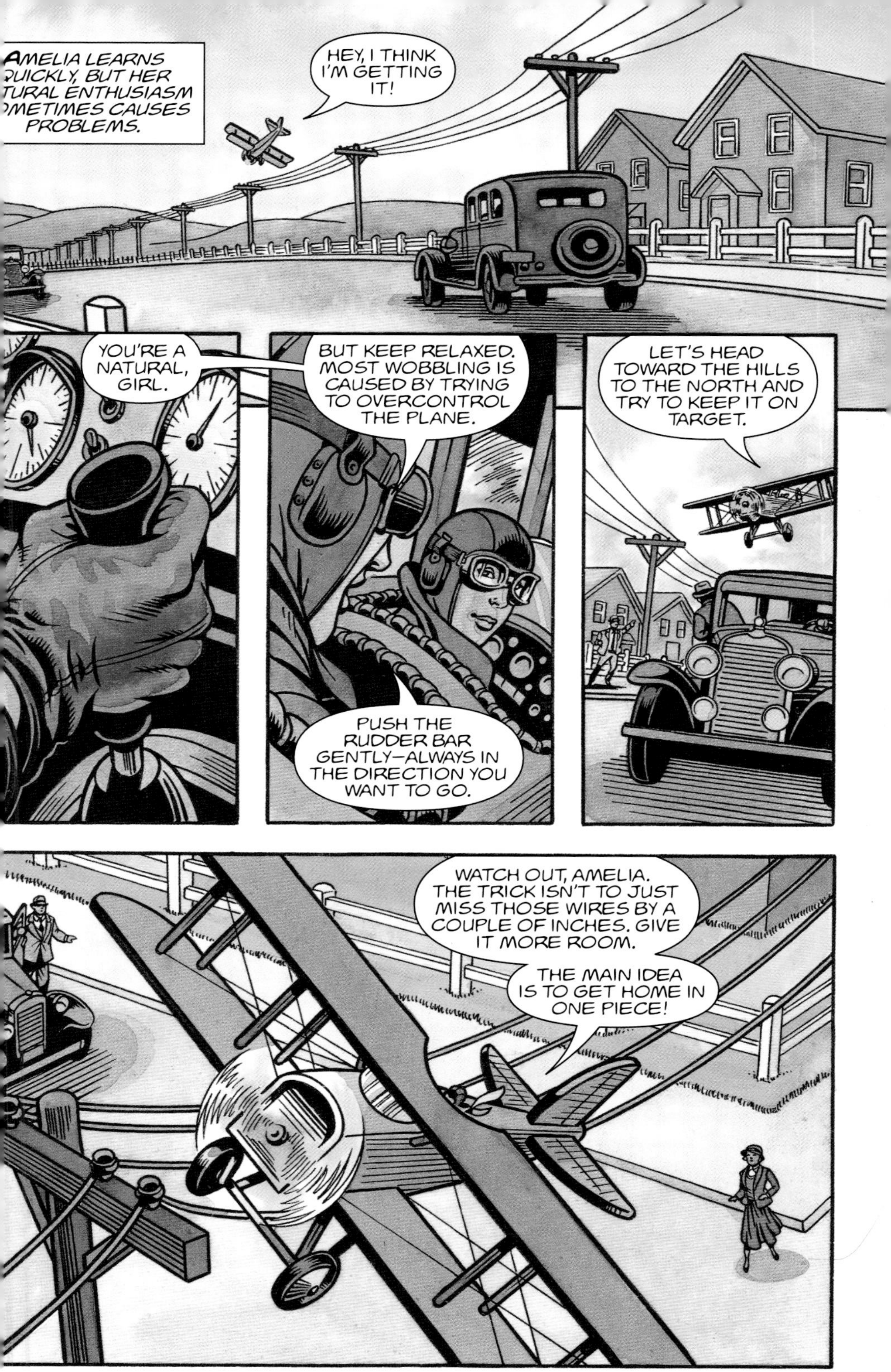
AMELIA LEARNS
UICKLY, BUT HER
TURAL ENTHUSIASM
METIMES CAUSES
PROBLEMS.
HEY, I THINK I'M GETTING IT!
YOU'RE A NATURAL, GIRL.
BUT KEEP RELAXED. MOST WOBBLING IS CAUSED BY TRYING TO OVERCONTROL THE PLANE.
PUSH THE RUDDER BAR GENTLY—ALWAYS IN THE DIRECTION YOU WANT TO GO.
LET'S HEAD TOWARD THE HILLS TO THE NORTH AND TRY TO KEEP IT ON TARGET.
WATCH OUT, AMELIA. THE TRICK ISN'T TO JUST MISS THOSE WIRES BY A COUPLE OF INCHES. GIVE IT MORE ROOM.
THE MAIN IDEA IS TO GET HOME IN ONE PIECE!

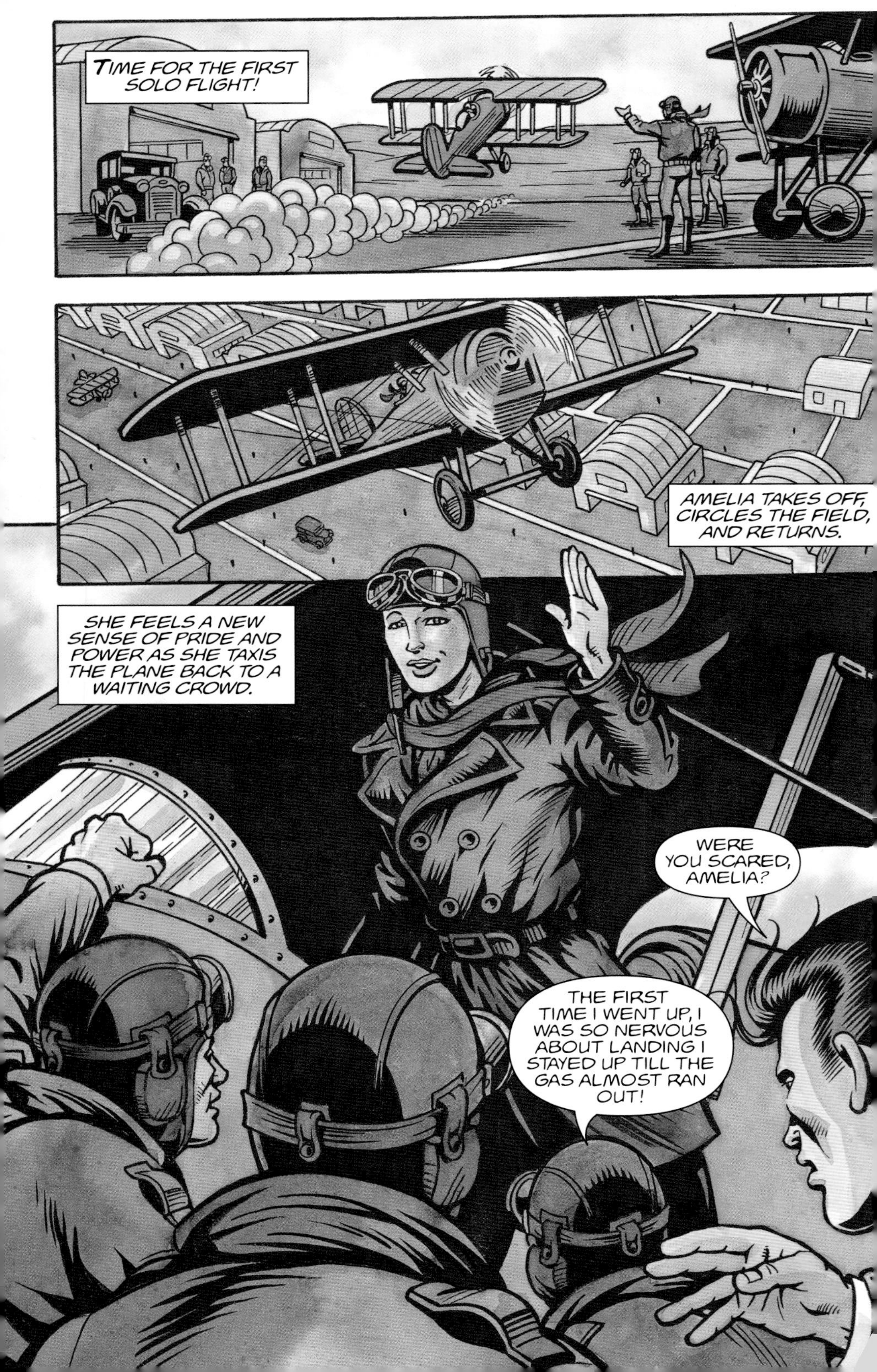
TIME FOR THE FIRST SOLO FLIGHT!
AMELIA TAKES OFF, CIRCLES THE FIELD, AND RETURNS.
SHE FEELS A NEW SENSE OF PRIDE AND POWER AS SHE TAXIS THE PLANE BACK TO A WAITING CROWD.
WERE YOU SCARED, AMELIA?
THE FIRST TIME I WENT UP, I WAS SO NERVOUS ABOUT LANDING I STAYED UP TILL THE GAS ALMOST RAN OUT!

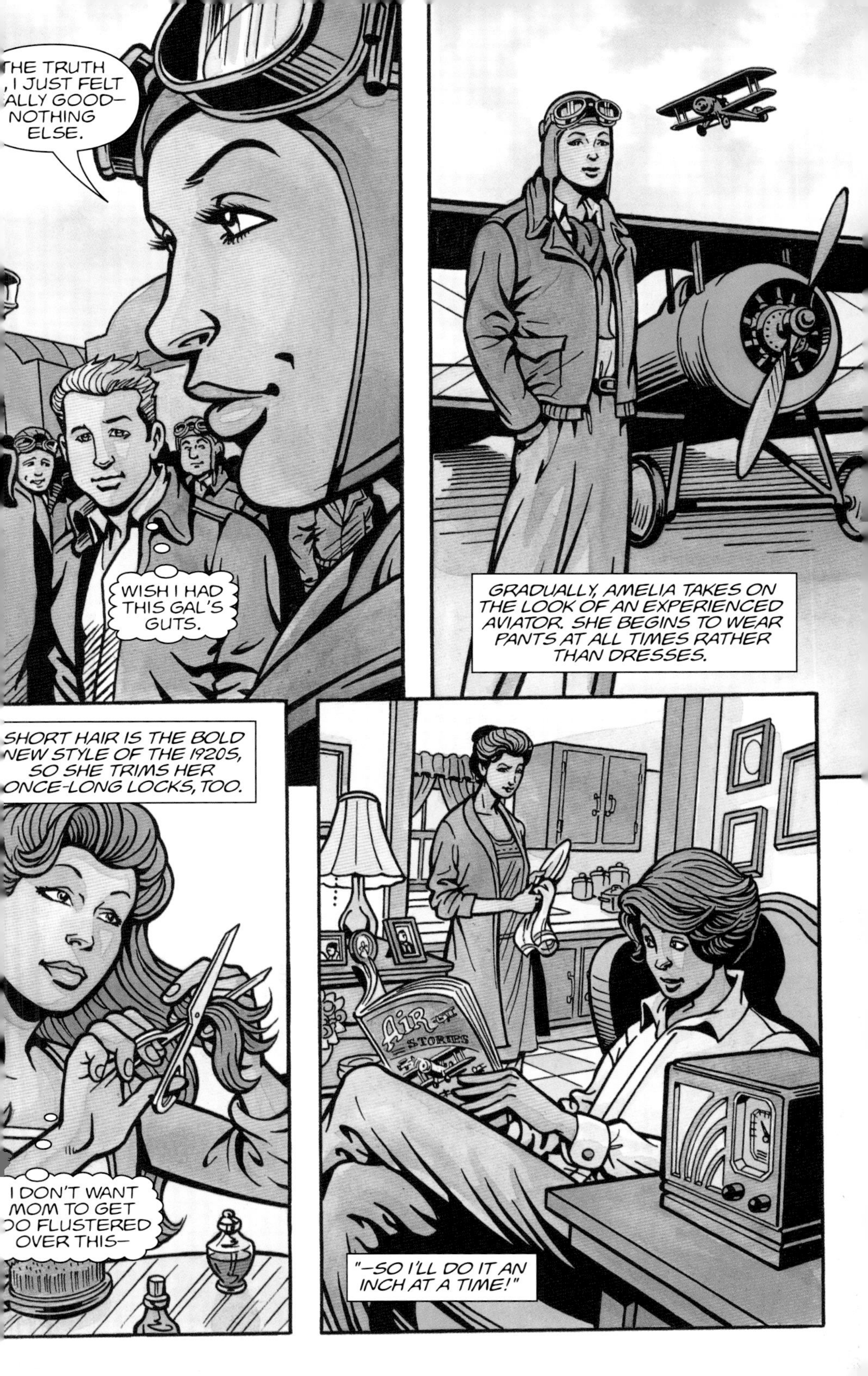
THE TRUTH
, I JUST FELT
ALLY GOOD—
NOTHING
ELSE.
WISH I HAD
THIS GAL'S
GUTS.
GRADUALLY, AMELIA TAKES ON
THE LOOK OF AN EXPERIENCED
AVIATOR. SHE BEGINS TO WEAR
PANTS AT ALL TIMES RATHER
THAN DRESSES.
SHORT HAIR IS THE BOLD
NEW STYLE OF THE 1920S,
SO SHE TRIMS HER
ONCE-LONG LOCKS, TOO.
I DON'T WANT
MOM TO GET
OO FLUSTERED
OVER THIS—
"—SO I'LL DO IT AN
INCH AT A TIME!"

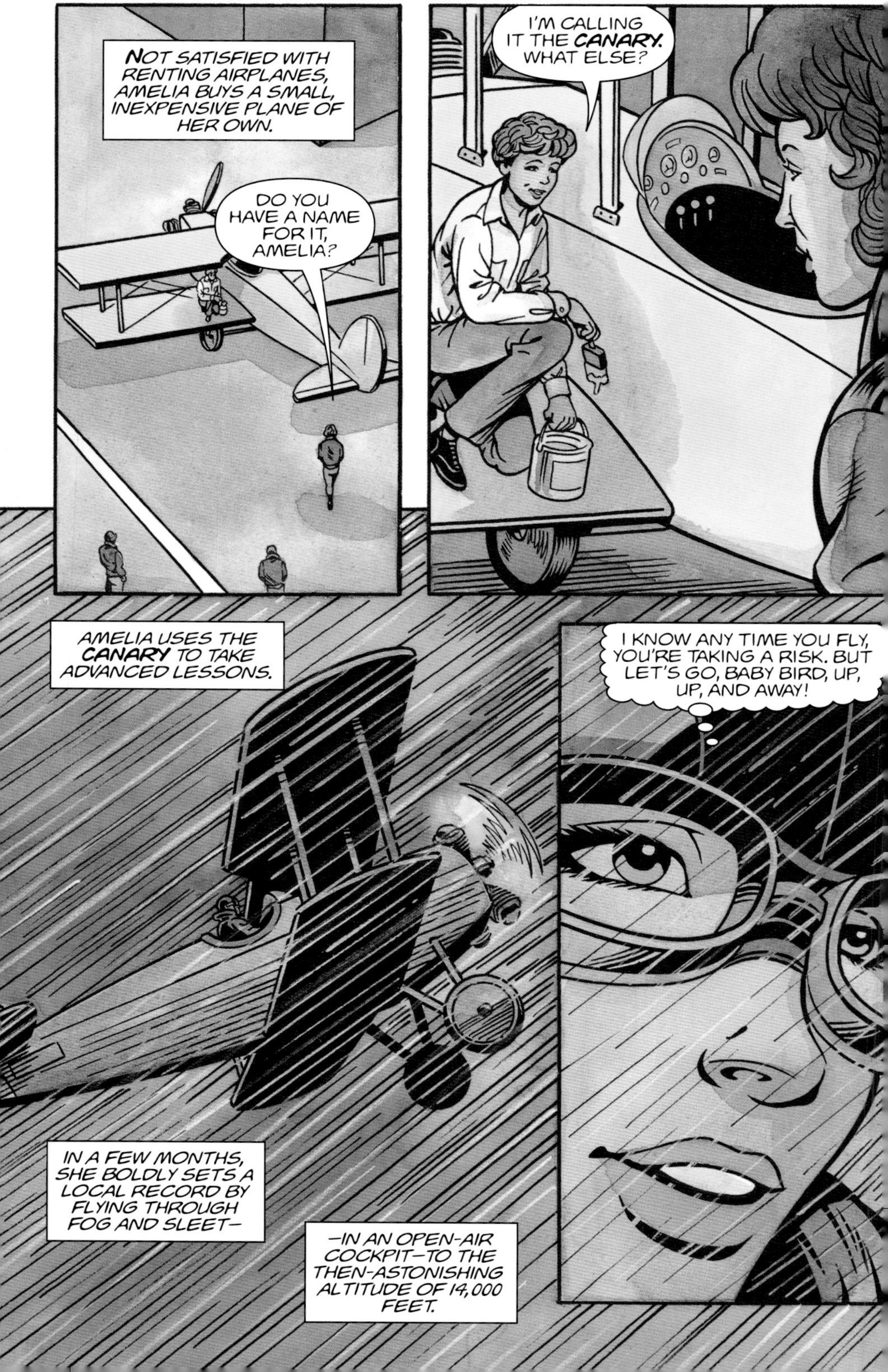
NOT SATISFIED WITH RENTING AIRPLANES, AMELIA BUYS A SMALL, INEXPENSIVE PLANE OF HER OWN.
DO YOU HAVE A NAME FOR IT, AMELIA?
I'M CALLING IT THE CANARY. WHAT ELSE?
AMELIA USES THE CANARY TO TAKE ADVANCED LESSONS.
I KNOW ANY TIME YOU FLY, YOU'RE TAKING A RISK. BUT LET'S GO, BABY BIRD, UP, UP, AND AWAY!
IN A FEW MONTHS, SHE BOLDLY SETS A LOCAL RECORD BY FLYING THROUGH FOG AND SLEET—
—IN AN OPEN-AIR COCKPIT—TO THE THEN-ASTONISHING ALTITUDE OF 14,000 FEET.

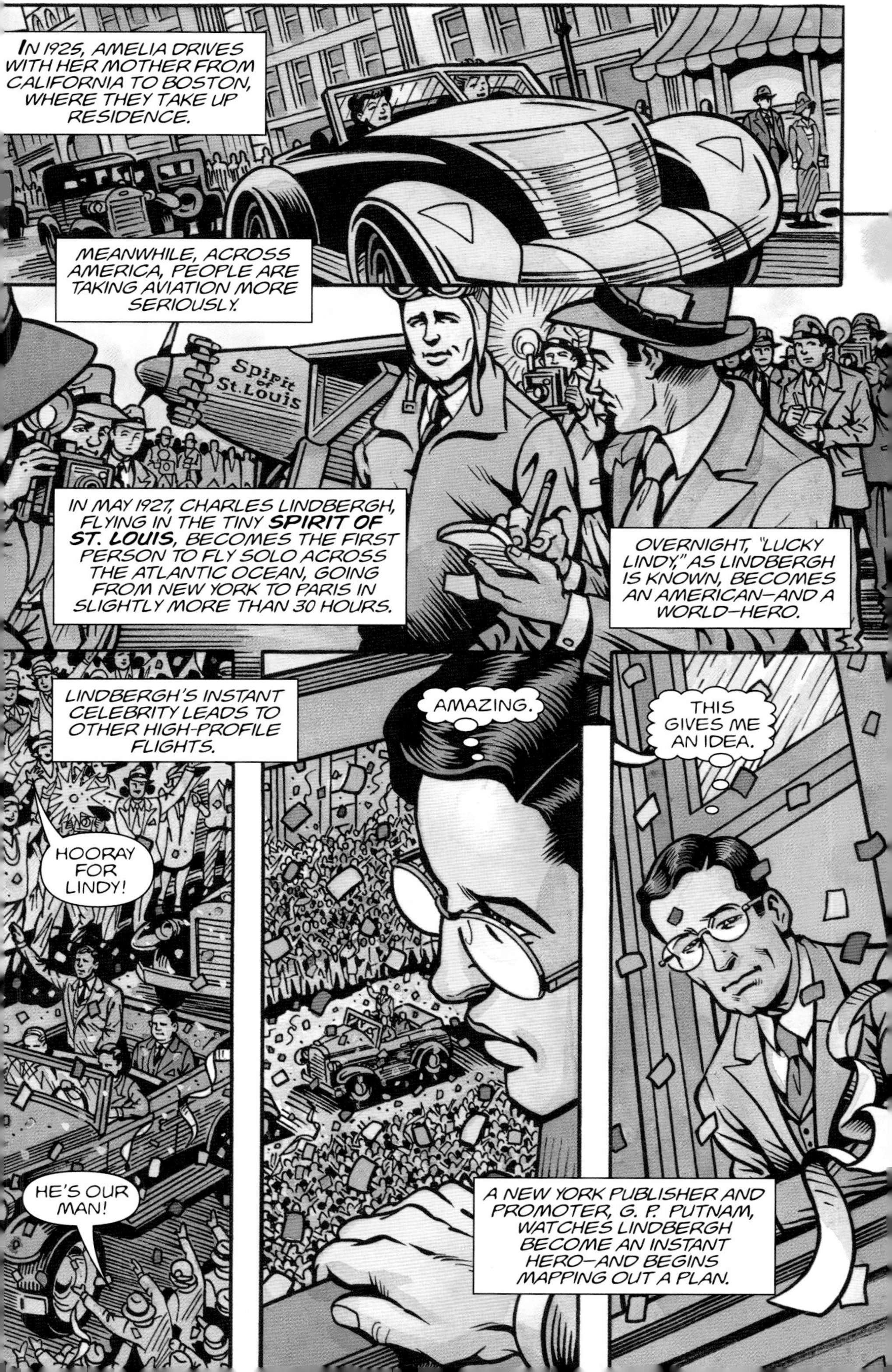
IN 1925, AMELIA DRIVES WITH HER MOTHER FROM CALIFORNIA TO BOSTON, WHERE THEY TAKE UP RESIDENCE.
MEANWHILE, ACROSS AMERICA, PEOPLE ARE TAKING AVIATION MORE SERIOUSLY.
Spirit of St. Louis
IN MAY 1927, CHARLES LINDBERGH, FLYING IN THE TINY **SPIRIT OF ST. LOUIS**, BECOMES THE FIRST PERSON TO FLY SOLO ACROSS THE ATLANTIC OCEAN, GOING FROM NEW YORK TO PARIS IN SLIGHTLY MORE THAN 30 HOURS.
OVERNIGHT, "LUCKY LINDY," AS LINDBERGH IS KNOWN, BECOMES AN AMERICAN—AND A WORLD—HERO.
LINDBERGH'S INSTANT CELEBRITY LEADS TO OTHER HIGH-PROFILE FLIGHTS.
HOORAY FOR LINDY!
HE'S OUR MAN!
AMAZING.
THIS GIVES ME AN IDEA.
A NEW YORK PUBLISHER AND PROMOTER, G. P. PUTNAM, WATCHES LINDBERGH BECOME AN INSTANT HERO—AND BEGINS MAPPING OUT A PLAN.

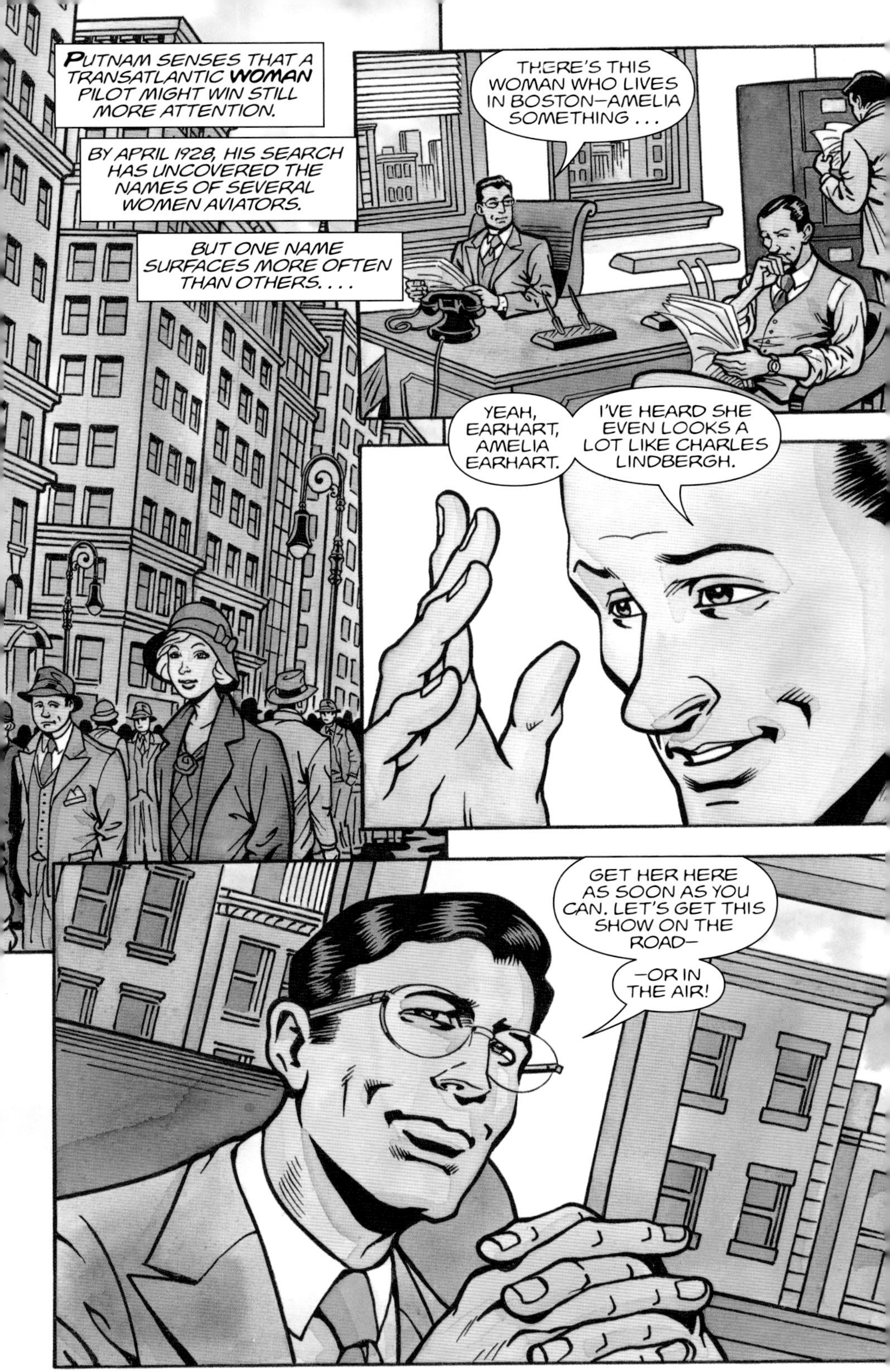
PUTNAM SENSES THAT A TRANSATLANTIC WOMAN PILOT MIGHT WIN STILL MORE ATTENTION.
BY APRIL 1928, HIS SEARCH HAS UNCOVERED THE NAMES OF SEVERAL WOMEN AVIATORS.
BUT ONE NAME SURFACES MORE OFTEN THAN OTHERS. . . .
THERE'S THIS WOMAN WHO LIVES IN BOSTON—AMELIA SOMETHING . . .
YEAH, EARHART, AMELIA EARHART.
I'VE HEARD SHE EVEN LOOKS A LOT LIKE CHARLES LINDBERGH.
GET HER HERE AS SOON AS YOU CAN. LET'S GET THIS SHOW ON THE ROAD—
—OR IN THE AIR!

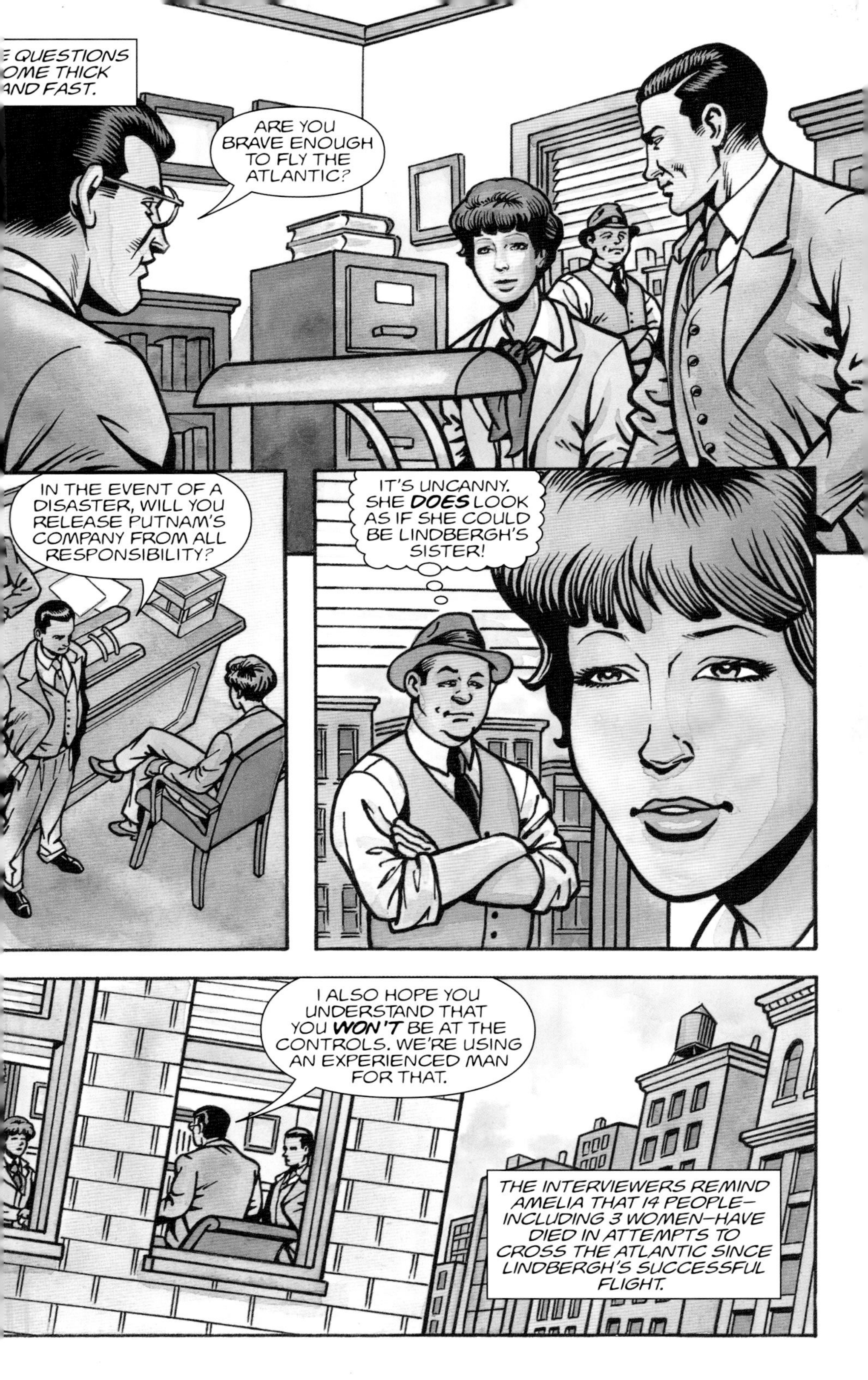
E QUESTIONS
OME THICK
AND FAST.
ARE YOU BRAVE ENOUGH TO FLY THE ATLANTIC?
IN THE EVENT OF A DISASTER, WILL YOU RELEASE PUTNAM'S COMPANY FROM ALL RESPONSIBILITY?
IT'S UNCANNY. SHE DOES LOOK AS IF SHE COULD BE LINDBERGH'S SISTER!
I ALSO HOPE YOU UNDERSTAND THAT YOU WON'T BE AT THE CONTROLS. WE'RE USING AN EXPERIENCED MAN FOR THAT.
THE INTERVIEWERS REMIND AMELIA THAT 14 PEOPLE–INCLUDING 3 WOMEN–HAVE DIED IN ATTEMPTS TO CROSS THE ATLANTIC SINCE LINDBERGH'S SUCCESSFUL FLIGHT.

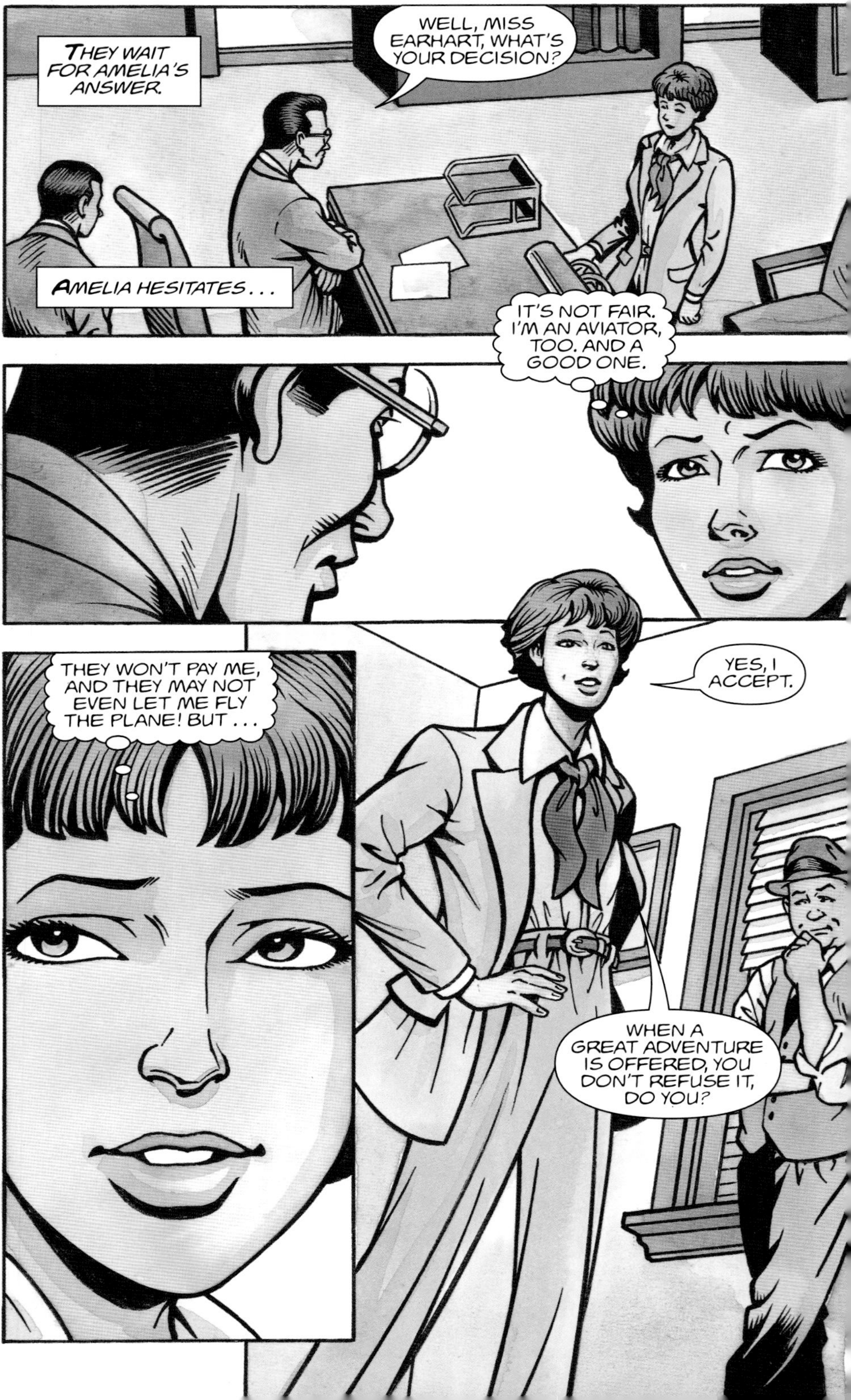
THEY WAIT FOR AMELIA'S ANSWER.
WELL, MISS EARHART, WHAT'S YOUR DECISION?
AMELIA HESITATES . . .
IT'S NOT FAIR. I'M AN AVIATOR, TOO. AND A GOOD ONE.
THEY WON'T PAY ME, AND THEY MAY NOT EVEN LET ME FLY THE PLANE! BUT . . .
YES, I ACCEPT.
WHEN A GREAT ADVENTURE IS OFFERED, YOU DON'T REFUSE IT, DO YOU?

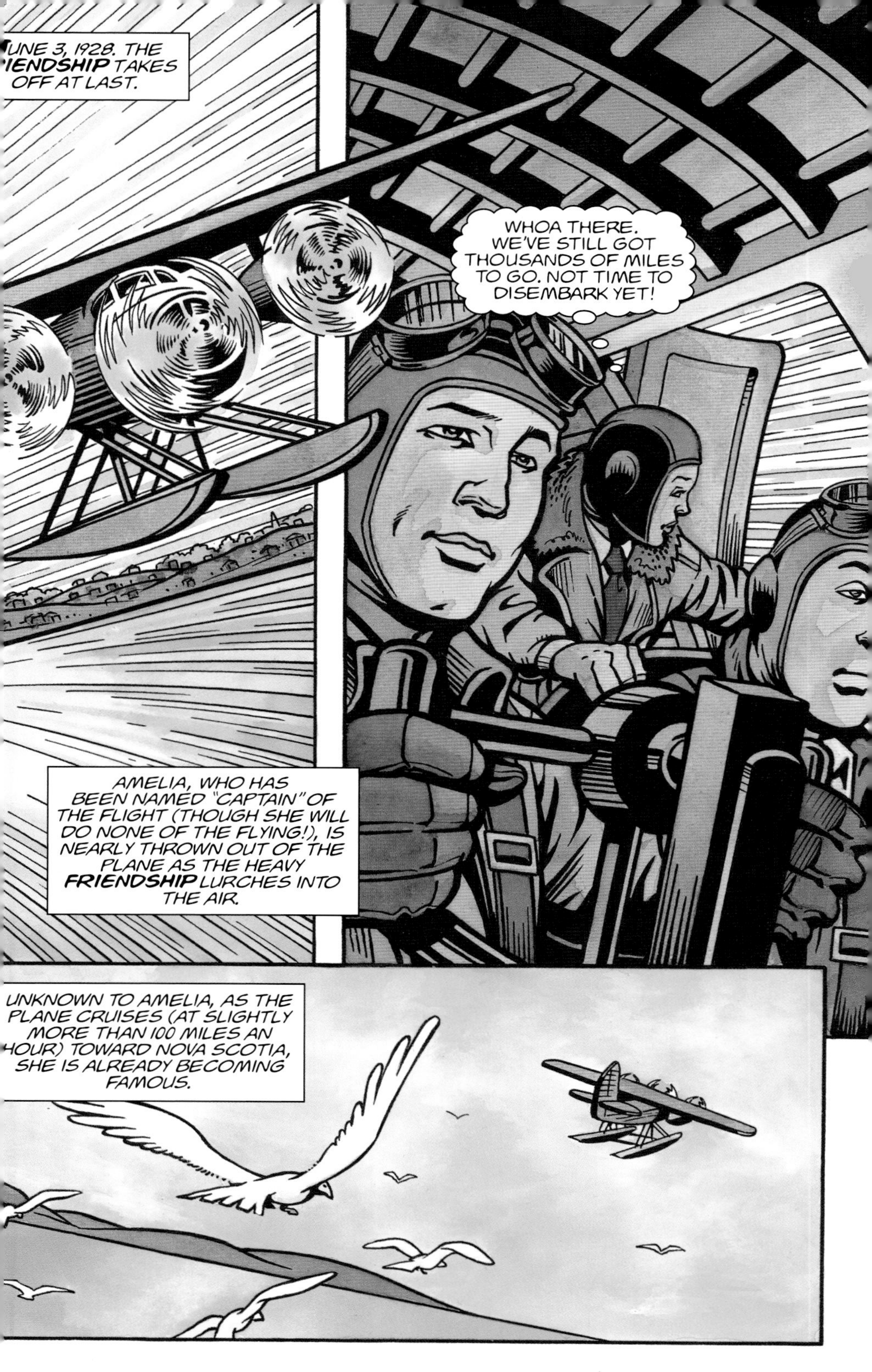
UNE 3, 1928. THE IENDSHIP TAKES OFF AT LAST.
WHOA THERE. WE'VE STILL GOT THOUSANDS OF MILES TO GO. NOT TIME TO DISEMBARK YET!
AMELIA, WHO HAS BEEN NAMED "CAPTAIN" OF THE FLIGHT (THOUGH SHE WILL DO NONE OF THE FLYING!), IS NEARLY THROWN OUT OF THE PLANE AS THE HEAVY FRIENDSHIP LURCHES INTO THE AIR.
UNKNOWN TO AMELIA, AS THE PLANE CRUISES (AT SLIGHTLY MORE THAN 100 MILES AN OUR) TOWARD NOVA SCOTIA, SHE IS ALREADY BECOMING FAMOUS.

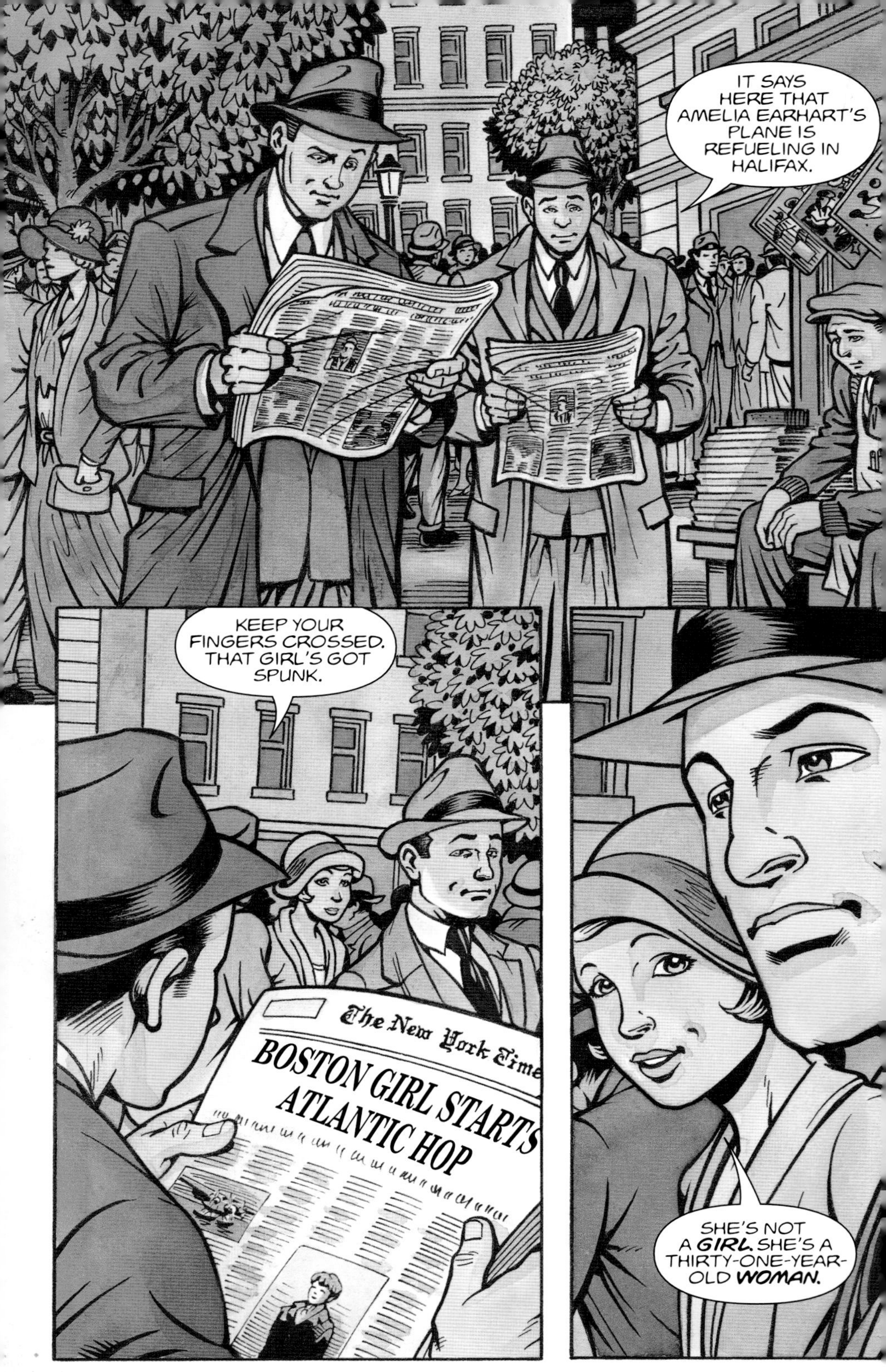
IT SAYS HERE THAT AMELIA EARHART'S PLANE IS REFUELING IN HALIFAX.
KEEP YOUR FINGERS CROSSED. THAT GIRL'S GOT SPUNK.
The New York Time
BOSTON GIRL STARTS ATLANTIC HOP
SHE'S NOT A **GIRL.** SHE'S A THIRTY-ONE-YEAR-OLD **WOMAN.**

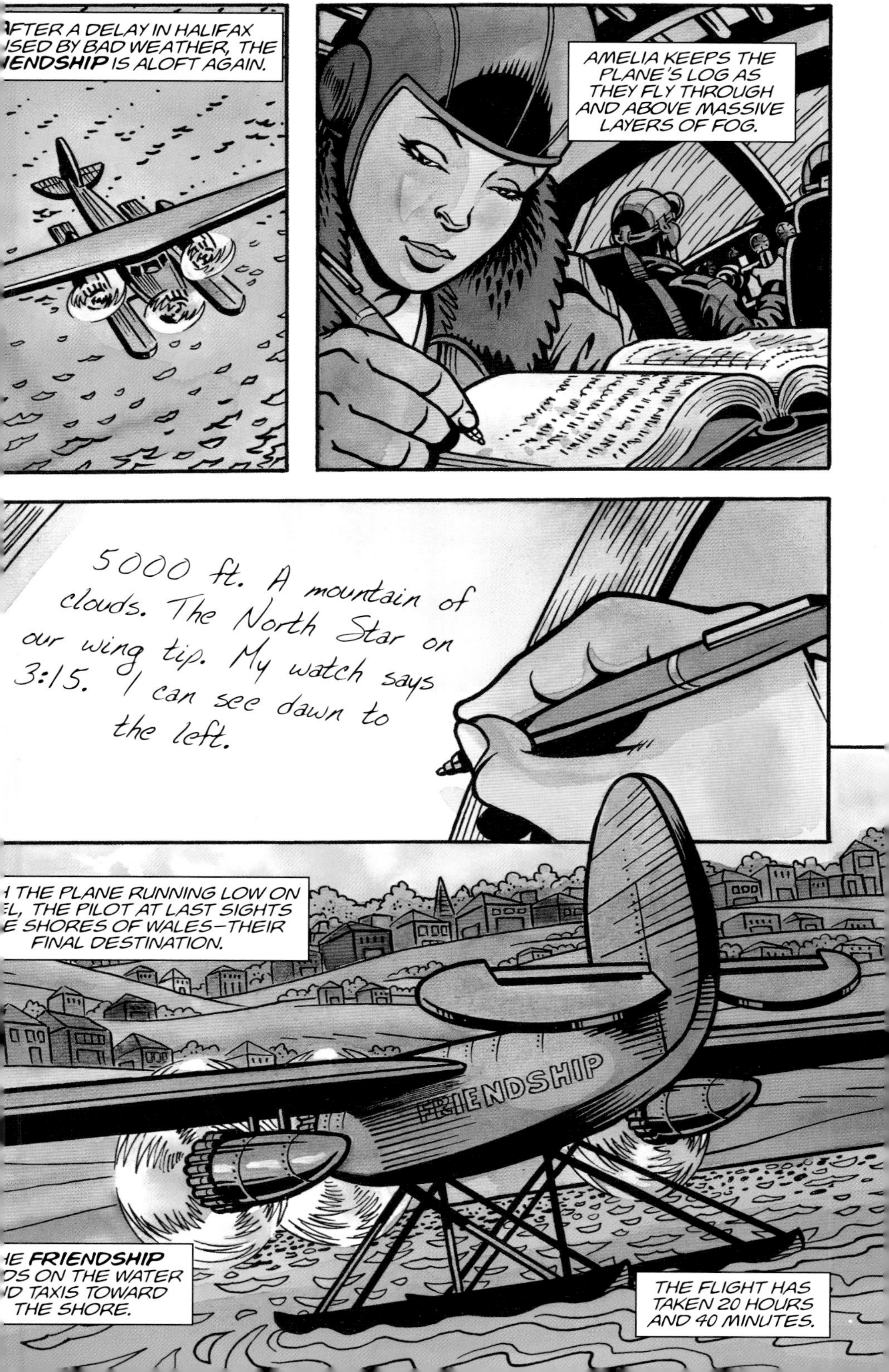
AFTER A DELAY IN HALIFAX
USED BY BAD WEATHER, THE
IENDSHIP IS ALOFT AGAIN.
AMELIA KEEPS THE PLANE'S LOG AS THEY FLY THROUGH AND ABOVE MASSIVE LAYERS OF FOG.
5000 ft. A mountain of clouds. The North Star on our wing tip. My watch says 3:15. I can see dawn to the left.
H THE PLANE RUNNING LOW ON
EL, THE PILOT AT LAST SIGHTS
E SHORES OF WALES—THEIR
FINAL DESTINATION.
FRIENDSHIP
HE FRIENDSHIP
DS ON THE WATER
ID TAXIS TOWARD
THE SHORE.
THE FLIGHT HAS TAKEN 20 HOURS AND 40 MINUTES.

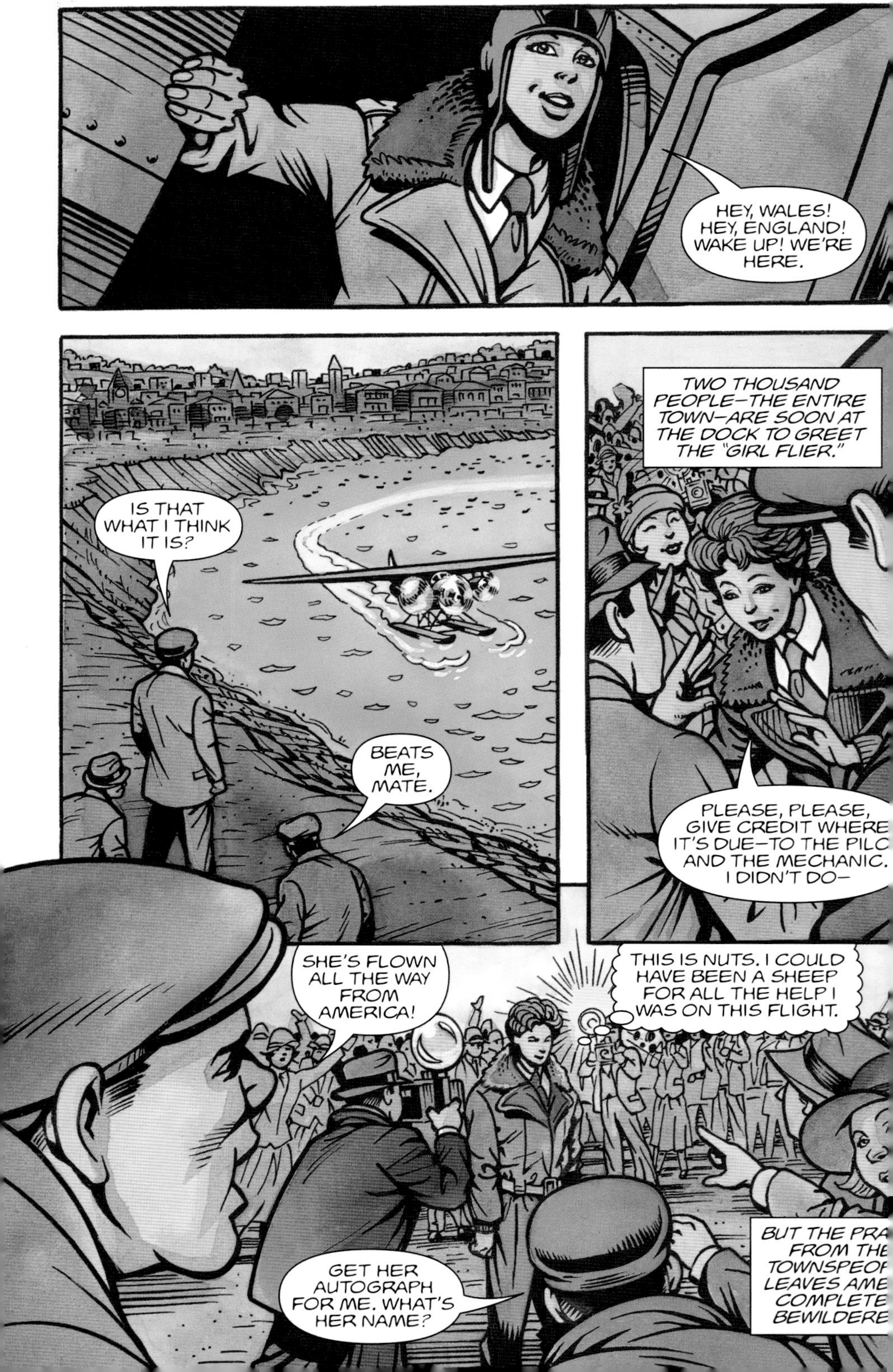
HEY, WALES! HEY, ENGLAND! WAKE UP! WE'RE HERE.
IS THAT WHAT I THINK IT IS?
BEATS ME, MATE.
TWO THOUSAND PEOPLE—THE ENTIRE TOWN—ARE SOON AT THE DOCK TO GREET THE "GIRL FLIER."
PLEASE, PLEASE, GIVE CREDIT WHERE IT'S DUE—TO THE PILO AND THE MECHANIC. I DIDN'T DO—
SHE'S FLOWN ALL THE WAY FROM AMERICA!
THIS IS NUTS. I COULD HAVE BEEN A SHEEP FOR ALL THE HELP I WAS ON THIS FLIGHT.
GET HER AUTOGRAPH FOR ME. WHAT'S HER NAME?
BUT THE PRA FROM THE TOWNSPEOF LEAVES AME COMPLETE BEWILDERE

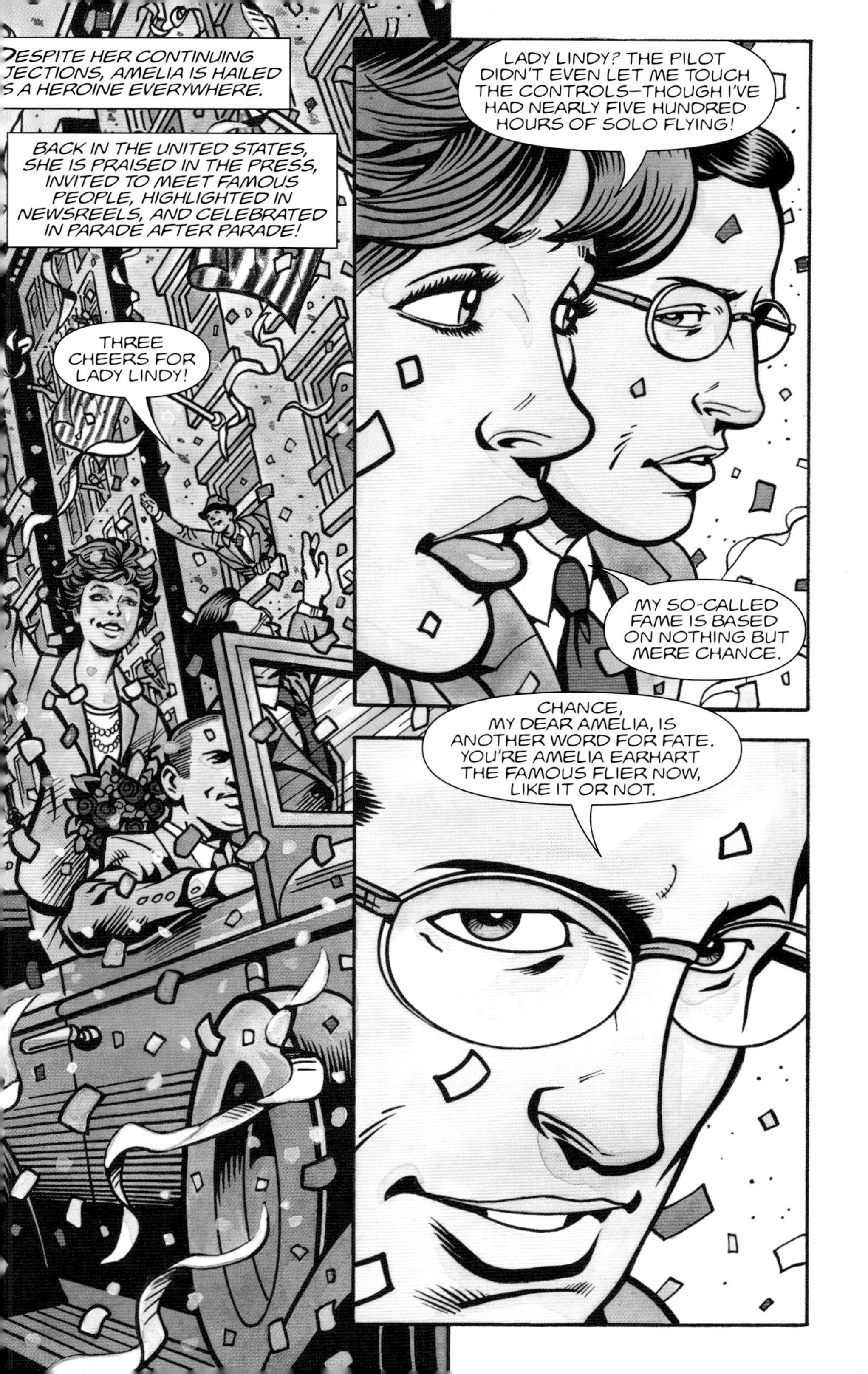
DESPITE HER CONTINUING JECTIONS, AMELIA IS HAILED S A HEROINE EVERYWHERE.
BACK IN THE UNITED STATES, SHE IS PRAISED IN THE PRESS, INVITED TO MEET FAMOUS PEOPLE, HIGHLIGHTED IN NEWSREELS, AND CELEBRATED IN PARADE AFTER PARADE!
THREE CHEERS FOR LADY LINDY!
LADY LINDY? THE PILOT DIDN'T EVEN LET ME TOUCH THE CONTROLS—THOUGH I'VE HAD NEARLY FIVE HUNDRED HOURS OF SOLO FLYING!
MY SO-CALLED FAME IS BASED ON NOTHING BUT MERE CHANCE.
CHANCE, MY DEAR AMELIA, IS ANOTHER WORD FOR FATE. YOU'RE AMELIA EARHART THE FAMOUS FLIER NOW, LIKE IT OR NOT.

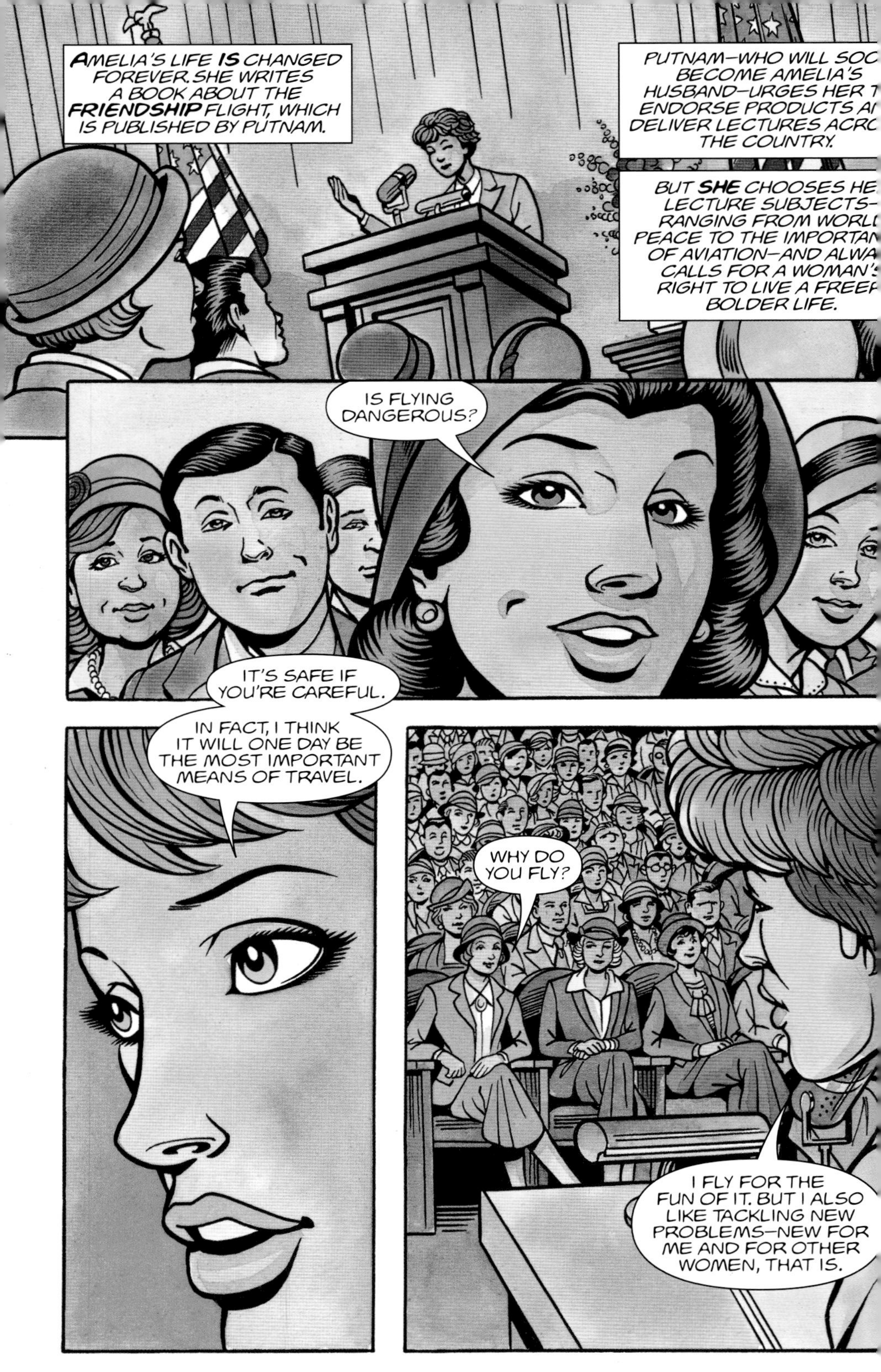
AMELIA'S LIFE IS CHANGED FOREVER. SHE WRITES A BOOK ABOUT THE FRIENDSHIP FLIGHT, WHICH IS PUBLISHED BY PUTNAM.
PUTNAM—WHO WILL SOO BECOME AMELIA'S HUSBAND—URGES HER T ENDORSE PRODUCTS A DELIVER LECTURES ACRO THE COUNTRY.
BUT SHE CHOOSES HE LECTURE SUBJECTS— RANGING FROM WORL PEACE TO THE IMPORTAN OF AVIATION—AND ALWA CALLS FOR A WOMAN'S RIGHT TO LIVE A FREEF BOLDER LIFE.
IS FLYING DANGEROUS?
IT'S SAFE IF YOU'RE CAREFUL.
IN FACT, I THINK IT WILL ONE DAY BE THE MOST IMPORTANT MEANS OF TRAVEL.
WHY DO YOU FLY?
I FLY FOR THE FUN OF IT. BUT I ALSO LIKE TACKLING NEW PROBLEMS—NEW FOR ME AND FOR OTHER WOMEN, THAT IS.

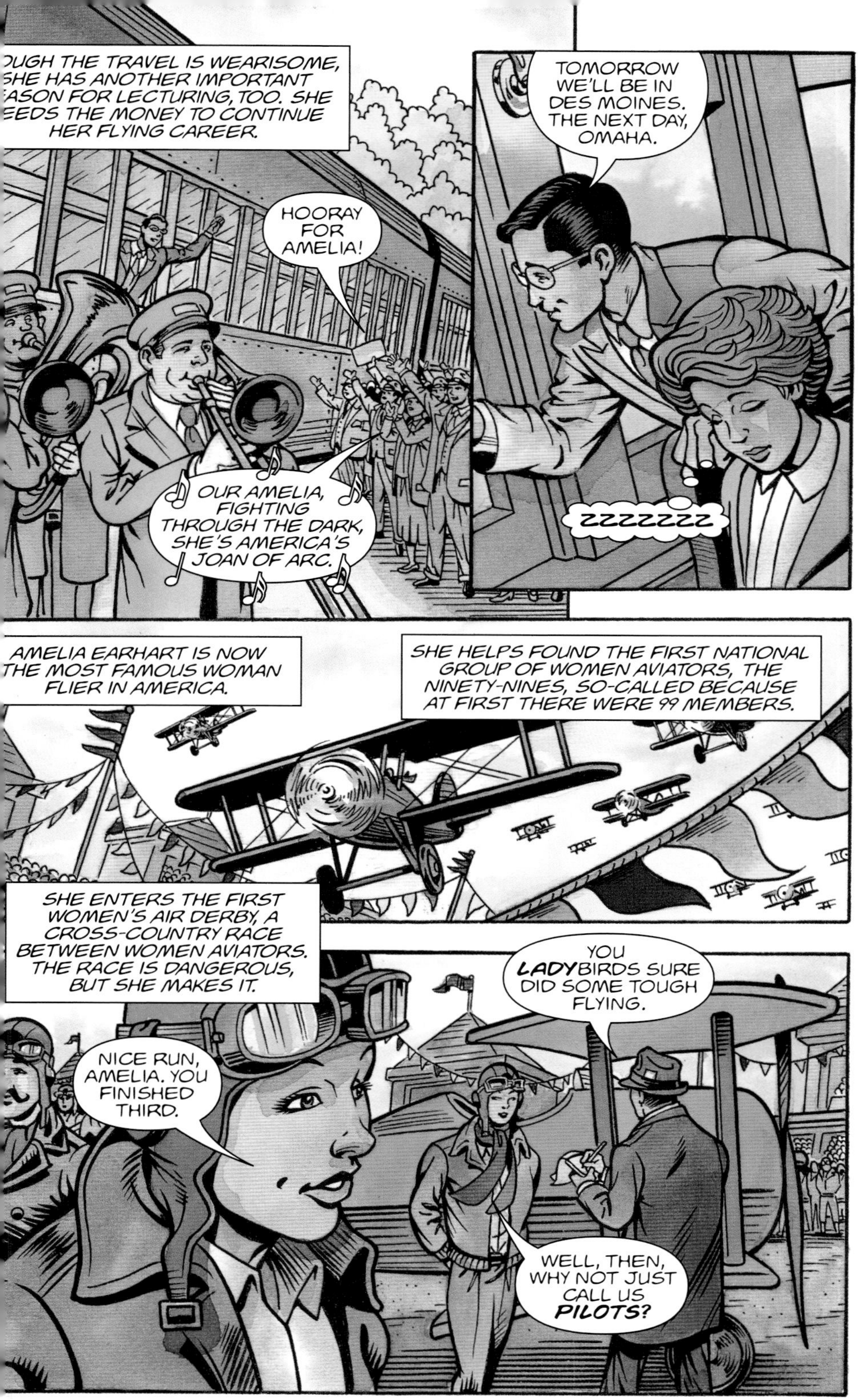
OUGH THE TRAVEL IS WEARISOME, SHE HAS ANOTHER IMPORTANT EASON FOR LECTURING, TOO. SHE EEDS THE MONEY TO CONTINUE HER FLYING CAREER.
HOORAY FOR AMELIA!
OUR AMELIA, FIGHTING THROUGH THE DARK, SHE'S AMERICA'S JOAN OF ARC.
TOMORROW WE'LL BE IN DES MOINES. THE NEXT DAY, OMAHA.
ZZZZZZZ
AMELIA EARHART IS NOW THE MOST FAMOUS WOMAN FLIER IN AMERICA.
SHE HELPS FOUND THE FIRST NATIONAL GROUP OF WOMEN AVIATORS, THE NINETY-NINES, SO-CALLED BECAUSE AT FIRST THERE WERE 99 MEMBERS.
SHE ENTERS THE FIRST WOMEN'S AIR DERBY, A CROSS-COUNTRY RACE BETWEEN WOMEN AVIATORS. THE RACE IS DANGEROUS, BUT SHE MAKES IT.
NICE RUN, AMELIA. YOU FINISHED THIRD.
YOU LADYBIRDS SURE DID SOME TOUGH FLYING.
WELL, THEN, WHY NOT JUST CALL US PILOTS?

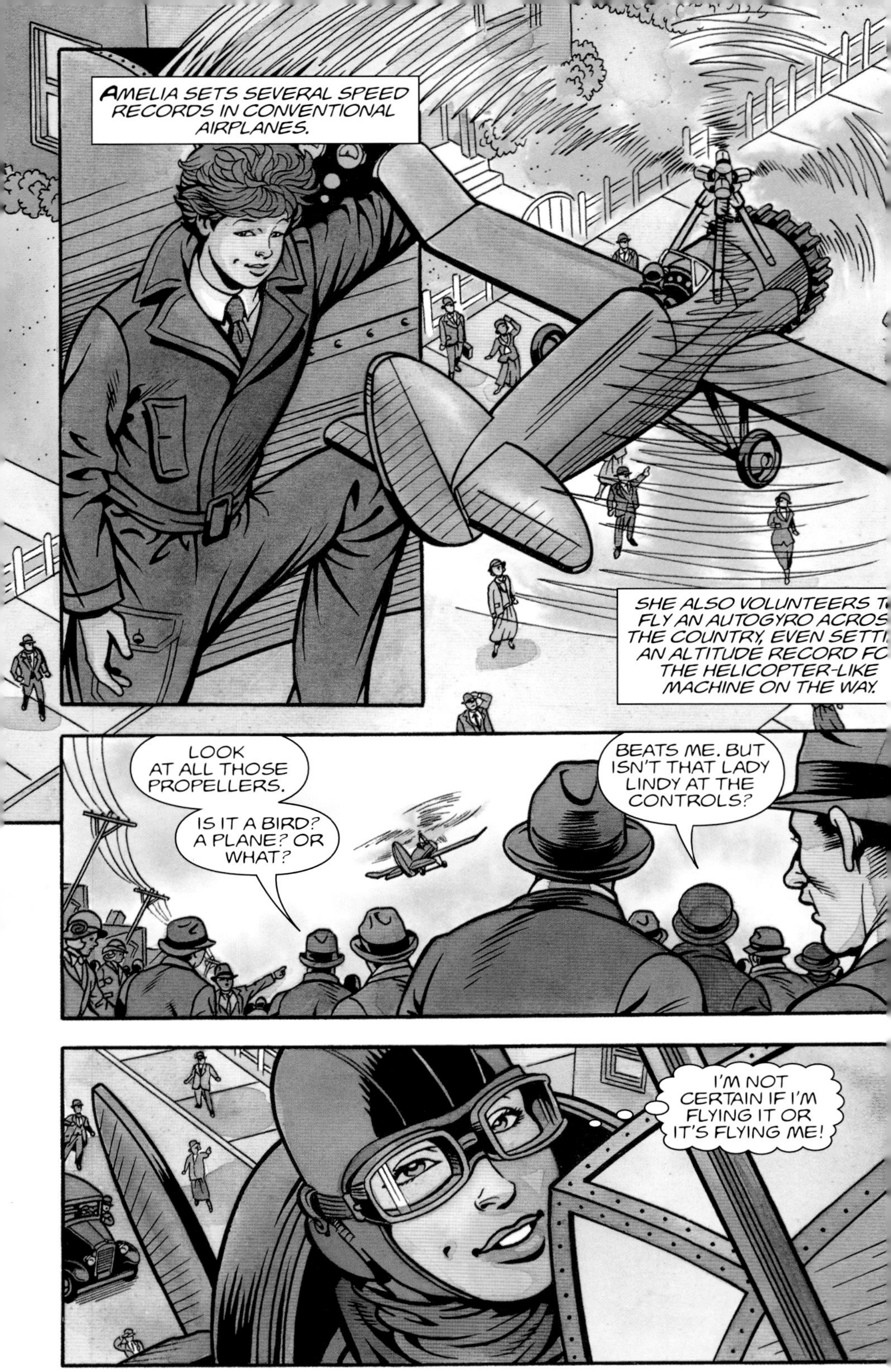
AMELIA SETS SEVERAL SPEED RECORDS IN CONVENTIONAL AIRPLANES.
SHE ALSO VOLUNTEERS T FLY AN AUTOGYRO ACROS THE COUNTRY, EVEN SETTI AN ALTITUDE RECORD FO THE HELICOPTER-LIKE MACHINE ON THE WAY.
LOOK AT ALL THOSE PROPELLERS.
IS IT A BIRD? A PLANE? OR WHAT?
BEATS ME. BUT ISN'T THAT LADY LINDY AT THE CONTROLS?
I'M NOT CERTAIN IF I'M FLYING IT OR IT'S FLYING ME!

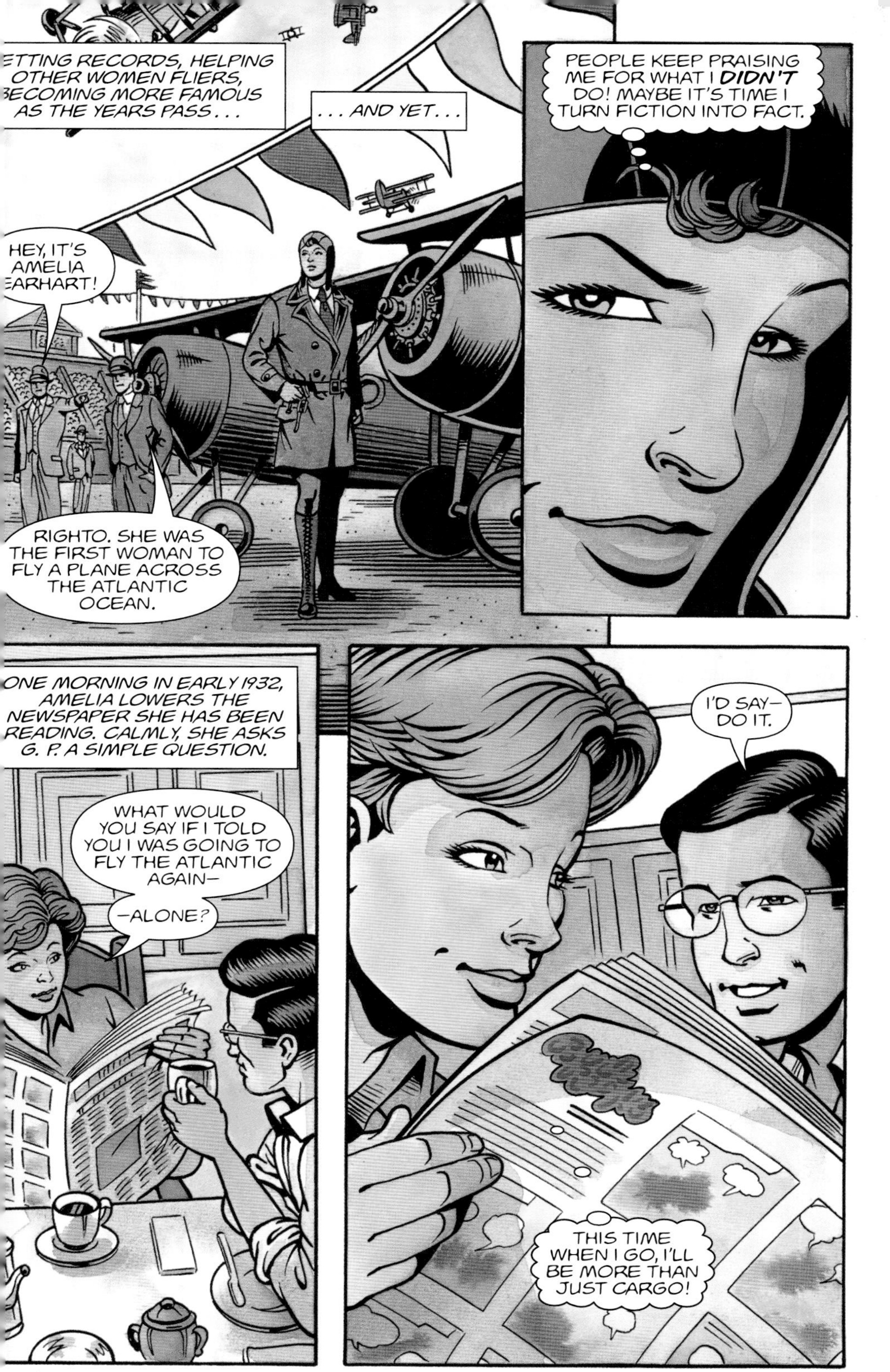

ETTING RECORDS, HELPING OTHER WOMEN FLIERS, BECOMING MORE FAMOUS AS THE YEARS PASS...
...AND YET...
HEY, IT'S AMELIA EARHART!
RIGHTO. SHE WAS THE FIRST WOMAN TO FLY A PLANE ACROSS THE ATLANTIC OCEAN.
PEOPLE KEEP PRAISING ME FOR WHAT I DIDN'T DO! MAYBE IT'S TIME I TURN FICTION INTO FACT.
ONE MORNING IN EARLY 1932, AMELIA LOWERS THE NEWSPAPER SHE HAS BEEN READING. CALMLY, SHE ASKS G. P. A SIMPLE QUESTION.
WHAT WOULD YOU SAY IF I TOLD YOU I WAS GOING TO FLY THE ATLANTIC AGAIN—
—ALONE?
I'D SAY— DO IT.
THIS TIME WHEN I GO, I'LL BE MORE THAN JUST CARGO!

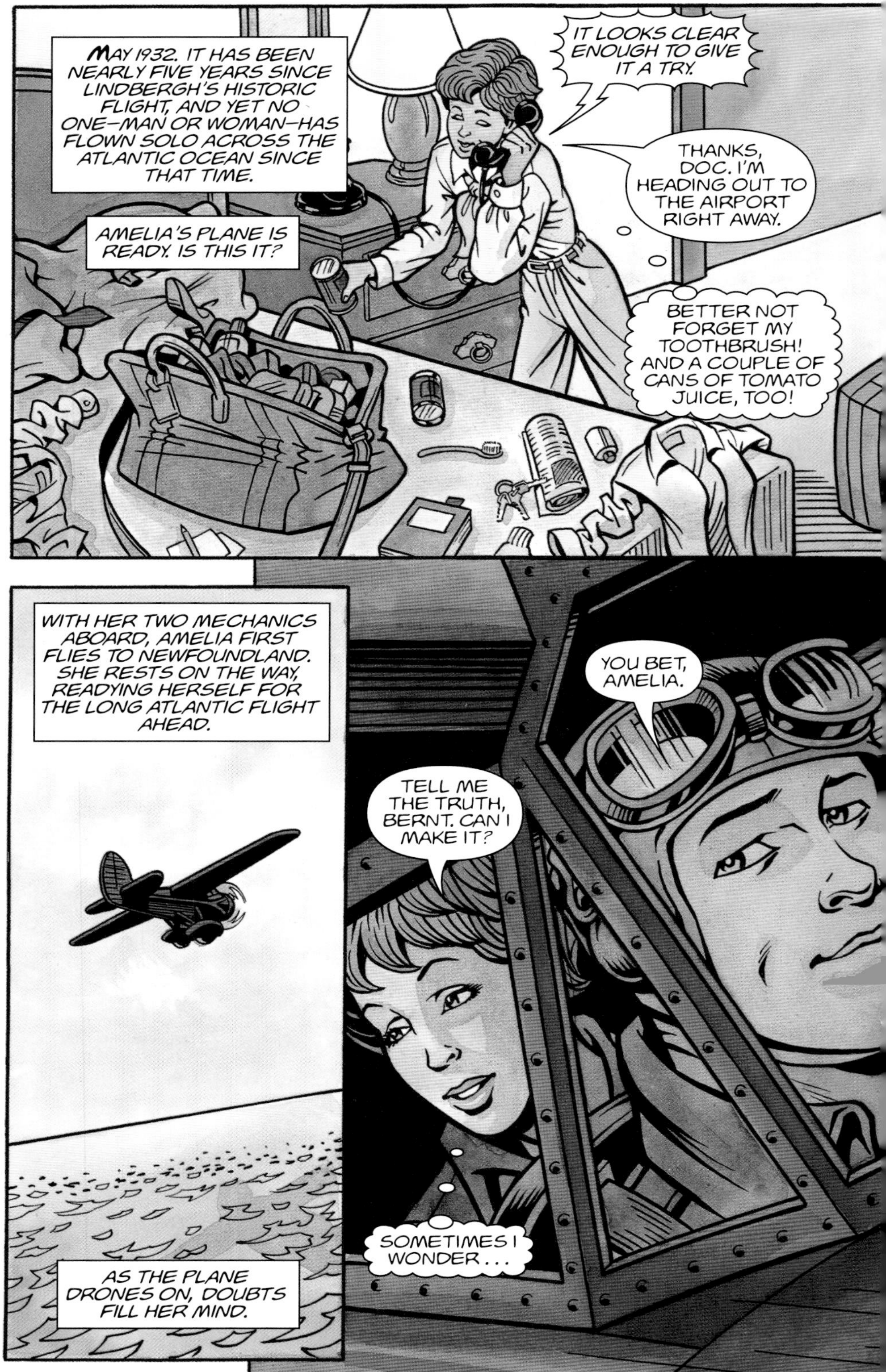
MAY 1932. IT HAS BEEN NEARLY FIVE YEARS SINCE LINDBERGH'S HISTORIC FLIGHT, AND YET NO ONE—MAN OR WOMAN—HAS FLOWN SOLO ACROSS THE ATLANTIC OCEAN SINCE THAT TIME.
IT LOOKS CLEAR ENOUGH TO GIVE IT A TRY.
THANKS, DOC. I'M HEADING OUT TO THE AIRPORT RIGHT AWAY.
AMELIA'S PLANE IS READY. IS THIS IT?
BETTER NOT FORGET MY TOOTHBRUSH! AND A COUPLE OF CANS OF TOMATO JUICE, TOO!
WITH HER TWO MECHANICS ABOARD, AMELIA FIRST FLIES TO NEWFOUNDLAND. SHE RESTS ON THE WAY, READYING HERSELF FOR THE LONG ATLANTIC FLIGHT AHEAD.
TELL ME THE TRUTH, BERNT. CAN I MAKE IT?
YOU BET, AMELIA.
SOMETIMES I WONDER . . .
AS THE PLANE DRONES ON, DOUBTS FILL HER MIND.

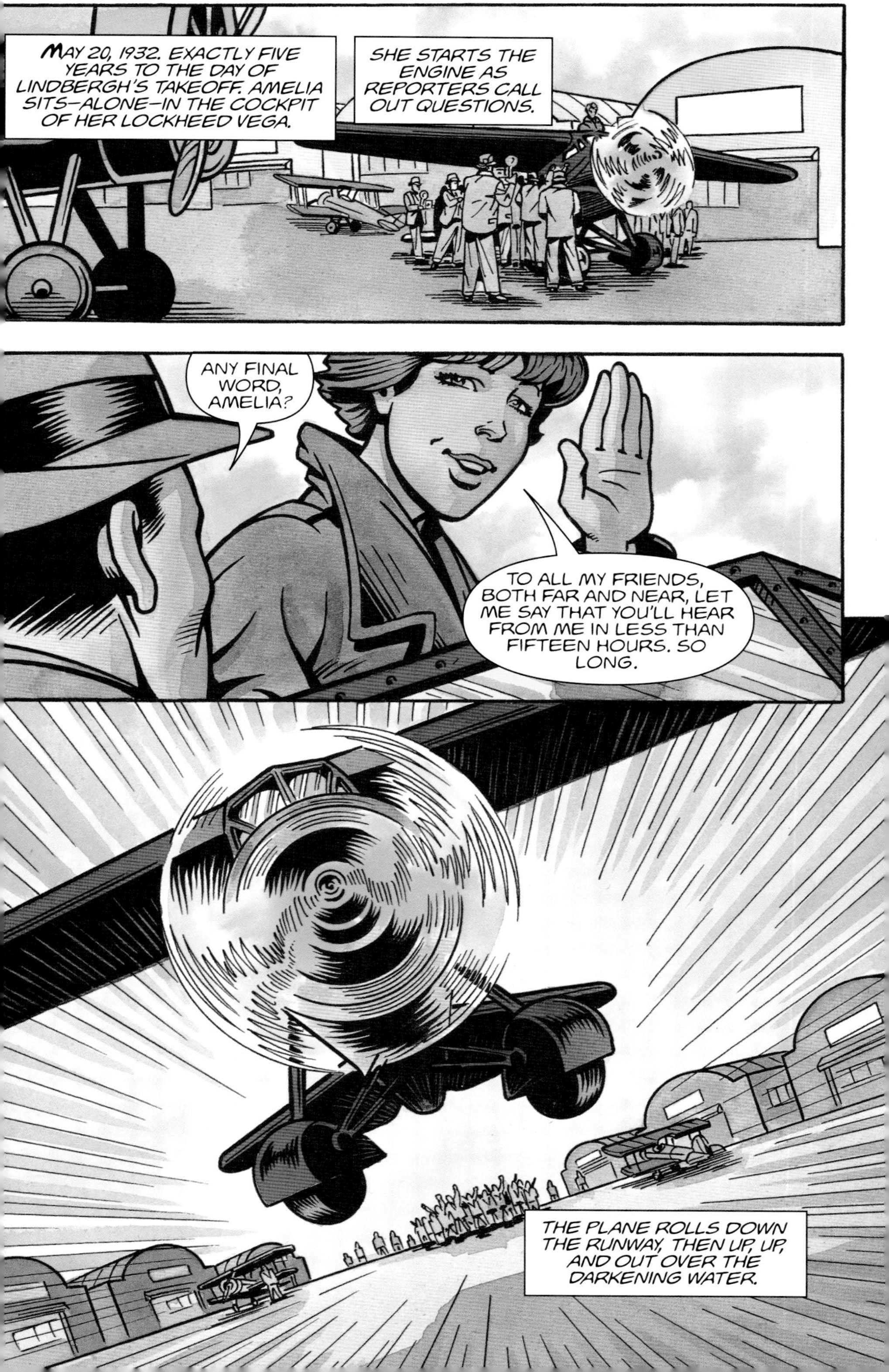
MAY 20, 1932. EXACTLY FIVE YEARS TO THE DAY OF LINDBERGH'S TAKEOFF. AMELIA SITS—ALONE—IN THE COCKPIT OF HER LOCKHEED VEGA.
SHE STARTS THE ENGINE AS REPORTERS CALL OUT QUESTIONS.
ANY FINAL WORD, AMELIA?
TO ALL MY FRIENDS, BOTH FAR AND NEAR, LET ME SAY THAT YOU'LL HEAR FROM ME IN LESS THAN FIFTEEN HOURS. SO LONG.
THE PLANE ROLLS DOWN THE RUNWAY, THEN UP, UP, AND OUT OVER THE DARKENING WATER.

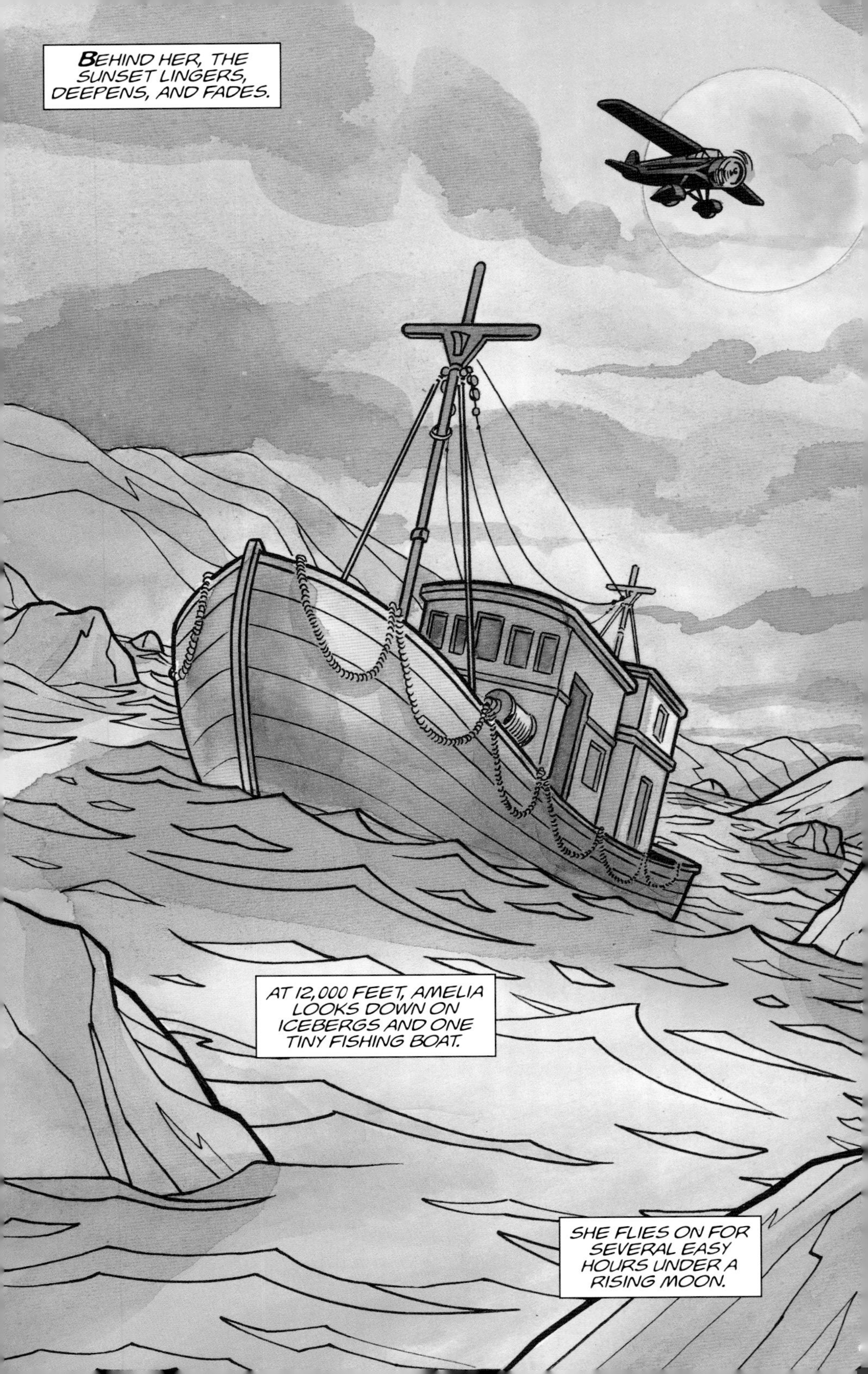
BEHIND HER, THE SUNSET LINGERS, DEEPENS, AND FADES.
AT 12,000 FEET, AMELIA LOOKS DOWN ON ICEBERGS AND ONE TINY FISHING BOAT.
SHE FLIES ON FOR SEVERAL EASY HOURS UNDER A RISING MOON.

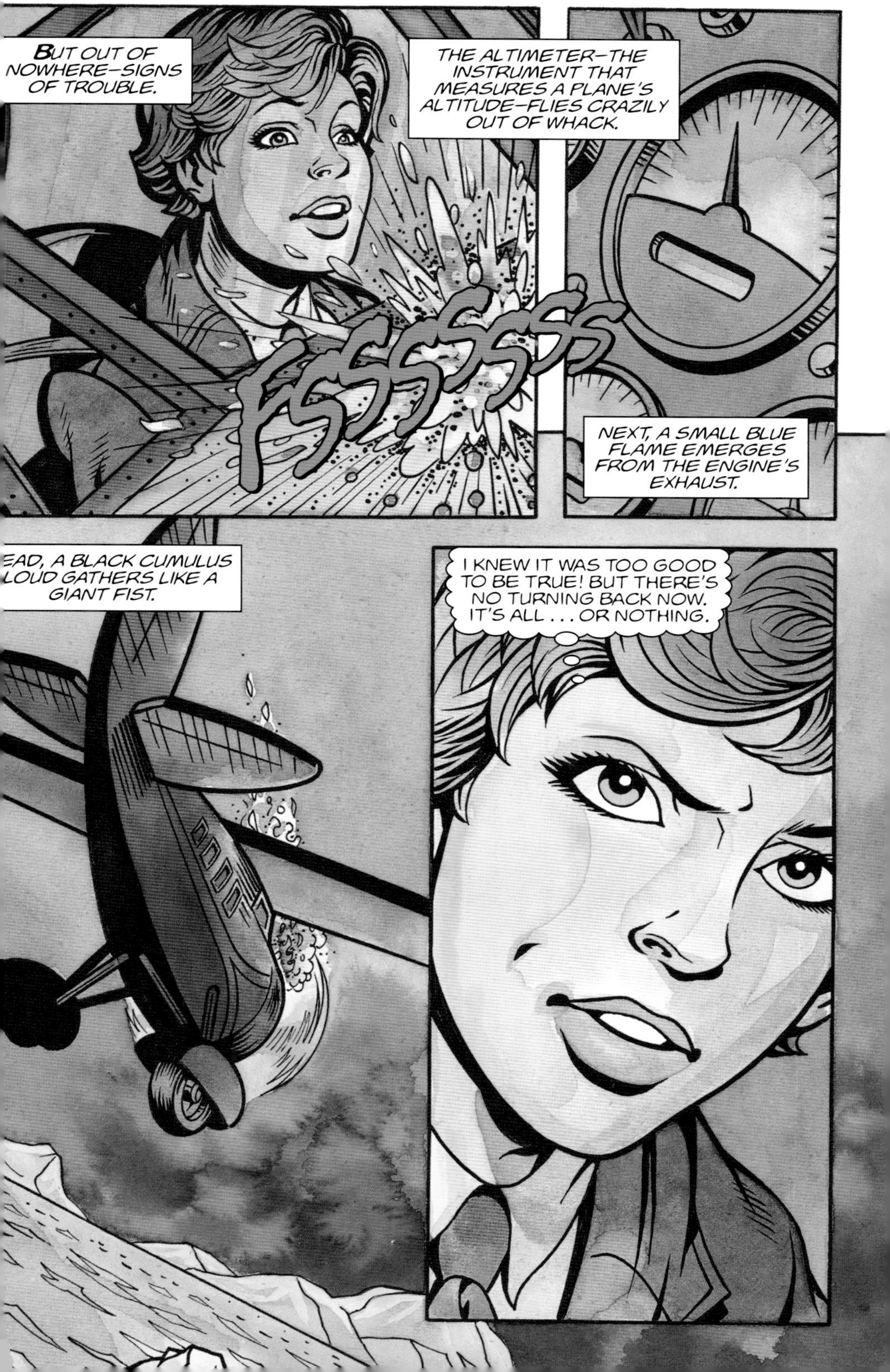
BUT OUT OF NOWHERE—SIGNS OF TROUBLE.
THE ALTIMETER—THE INSTRUMENT THAT MEASURES A PLANE'S ALTITUDE—FLIES CRAZILY OUT OF WHACK.
FSSSSSSS
NEXT, A SMALL BLUE FLAME EMERGES FROM THE ENGINE'S EXHAUST.
EAD, A BLACK CUMULUS LOUD GATHERS LIKE A GIANT FIST.
I KNEW IT WAS TOO GOOD TO BE TRUE! BUT THERE'S NO TURNING BACK NOW. IT'S ALL . . . OR NOTHING.

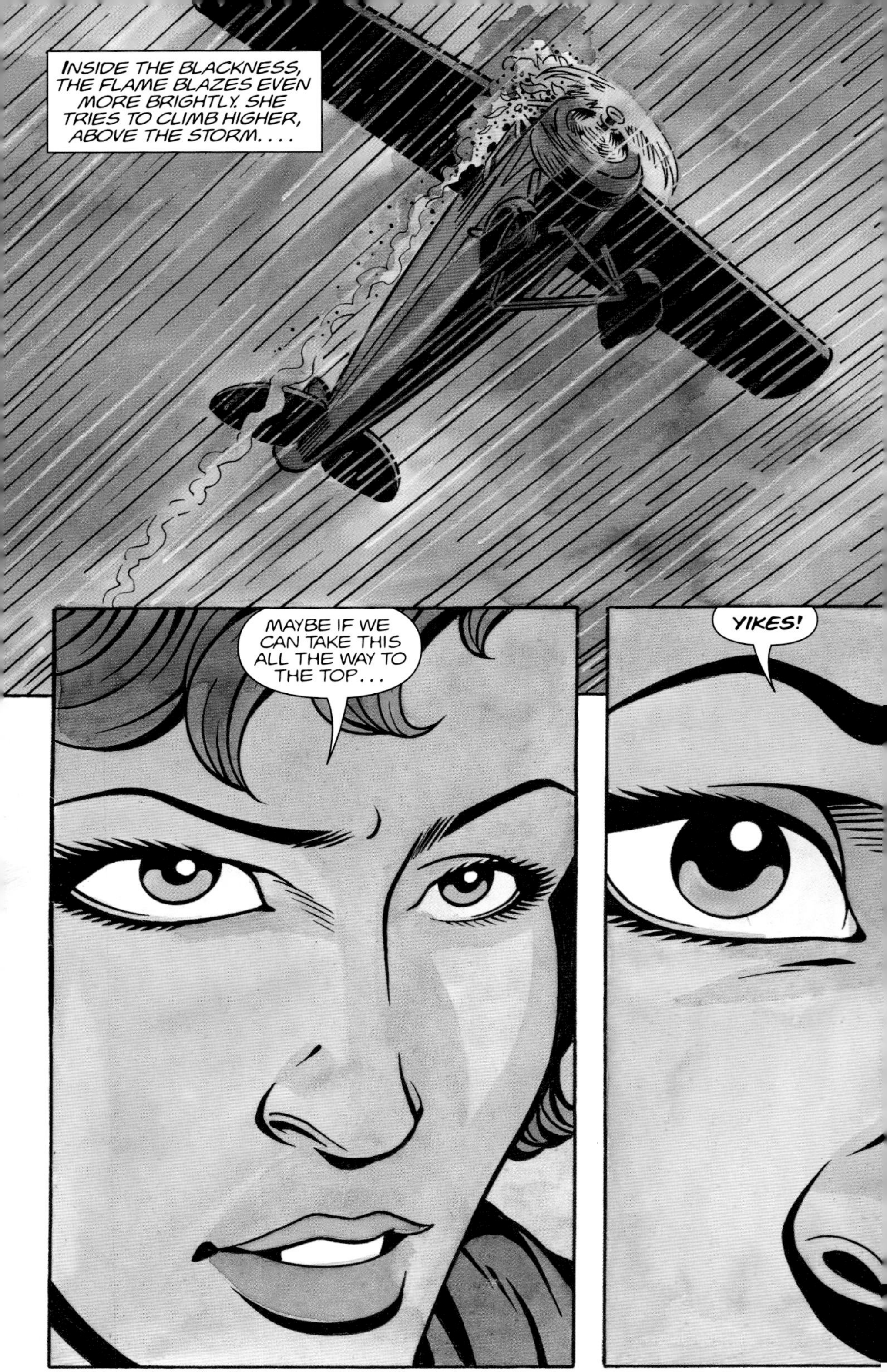
INSIDE THE BLACKNESS, THE FLAME BLAZES EVEN MORE BRIGHTLY. SHE TRIES TO CLIMB HIGHER, ABOVE THE STORM. . . .
MAYBE IF WE CAN TAKE THIS ALL THE WAY TO THE TOP . . .
YIKES!

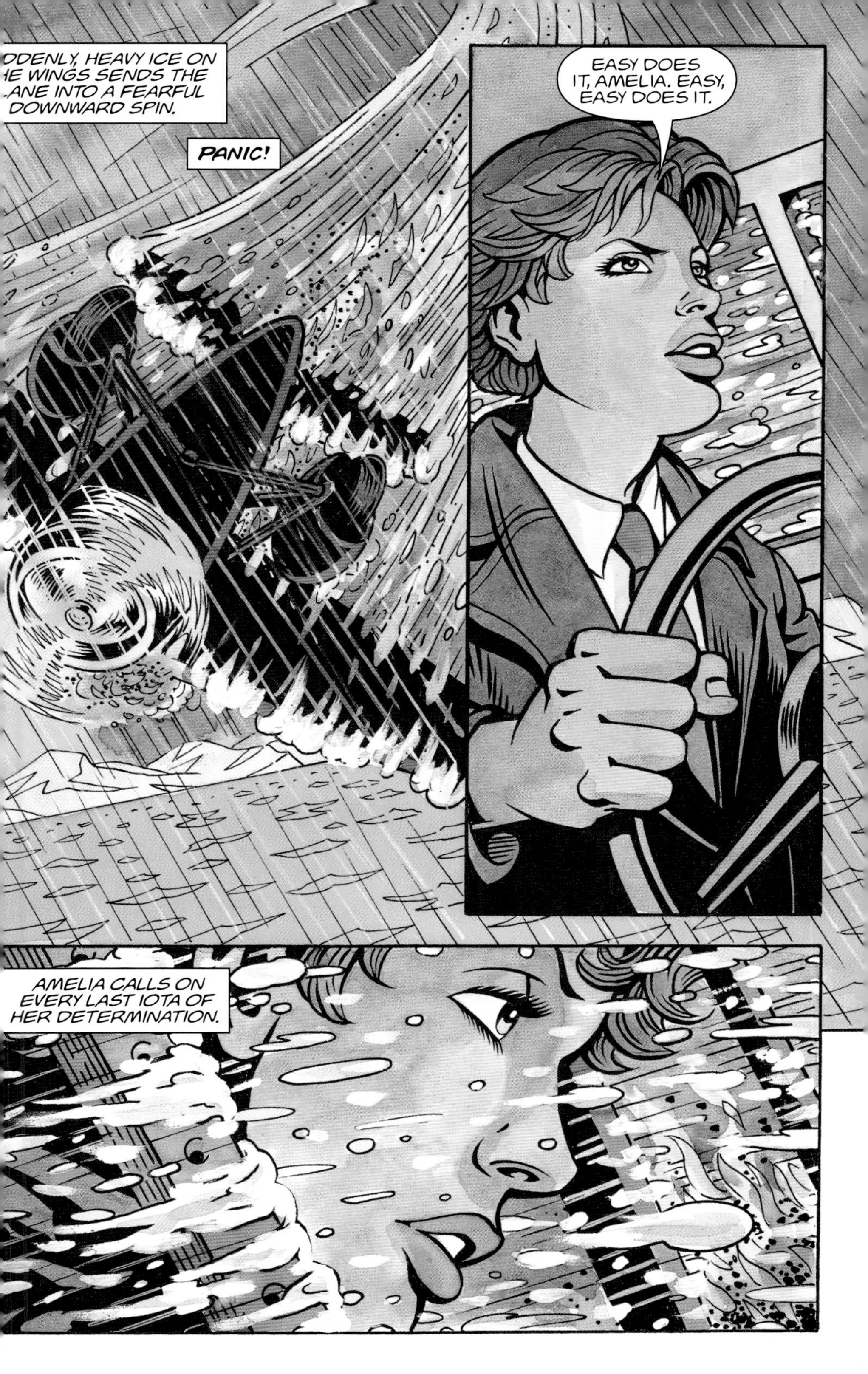
DDENLY, HEAVY ICE ON
HE WINGS SENDS THE
ANE INTO A FEARFUL
DOWNWARD SPIN.
PANIC!
EASY DOES IT, AMELIA. EASY, EASY DOES IT.
AMELIA CALLS ON EVERY LAST IOTA OF HER DETERMINATION.

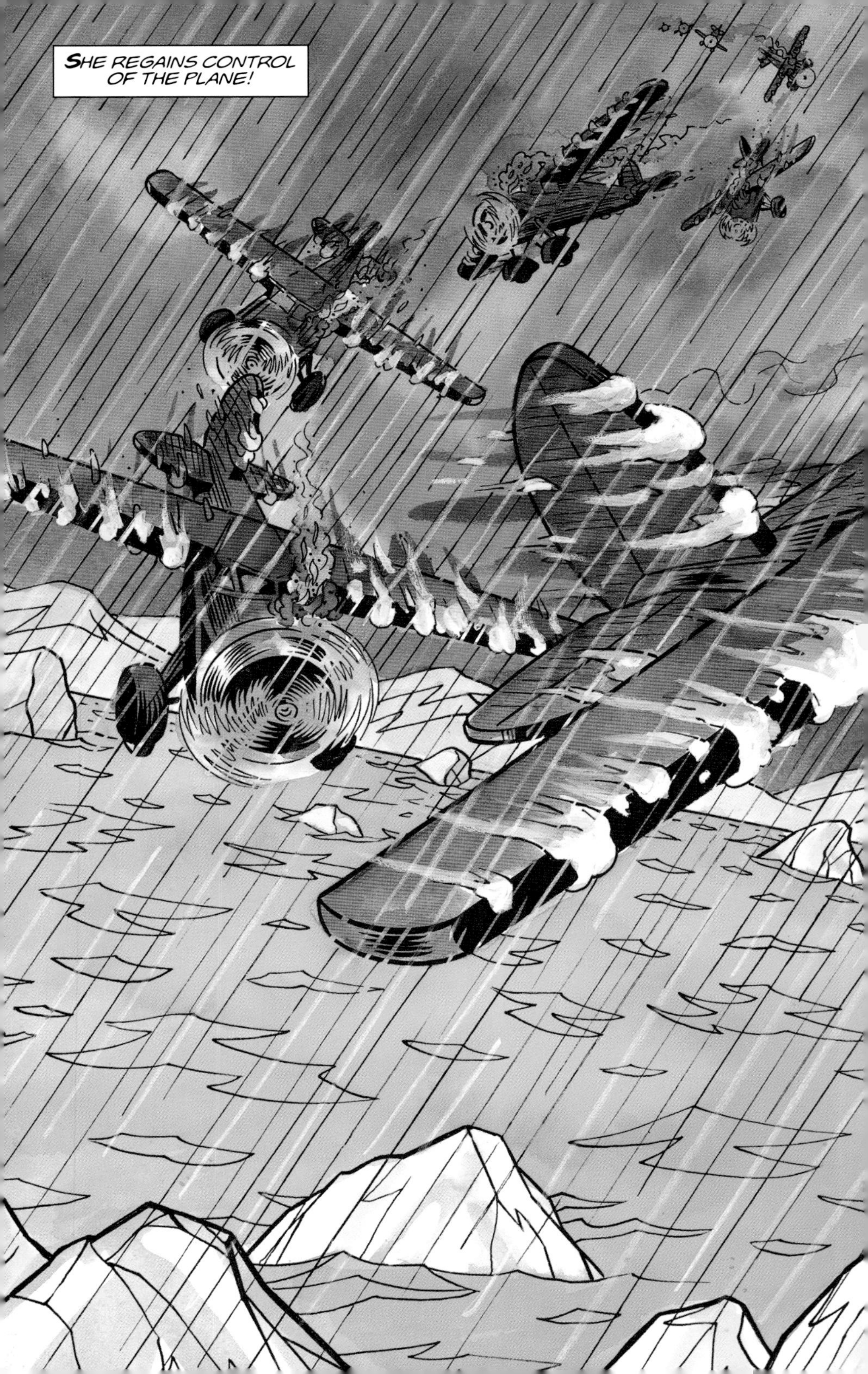
SHE REGAINS CONTROL OF THE PLANE!

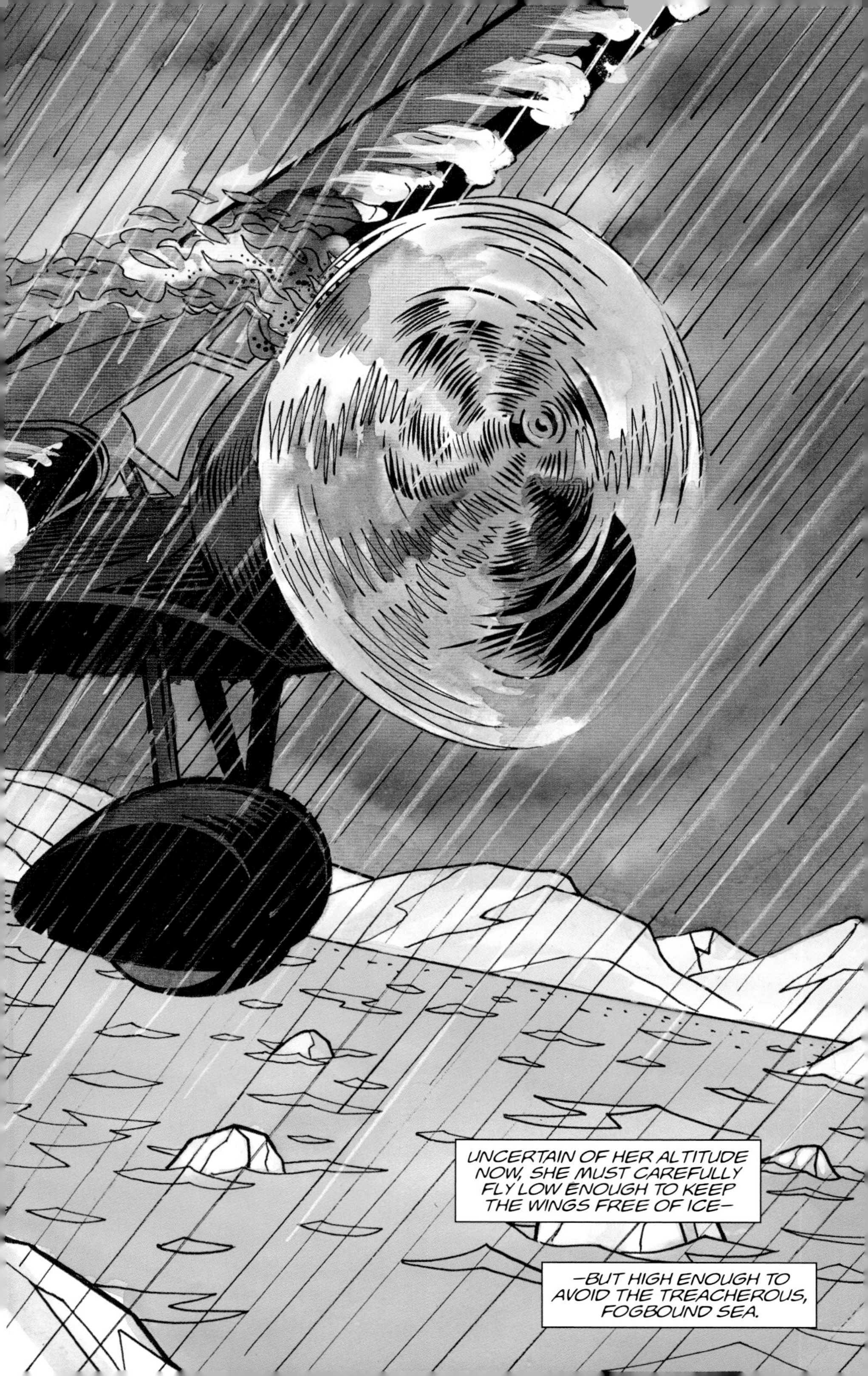
UNCERTAIN OF HER ALTITUDE NOW, SHE MUST CAREFULLY FLY LOW ENOUGH TO KEEP THE WINGS FREE OF ICE—
—BUT HIGH ENOUGH TO AVOID THE TREACHEROUS, FOGBOUND SEA.

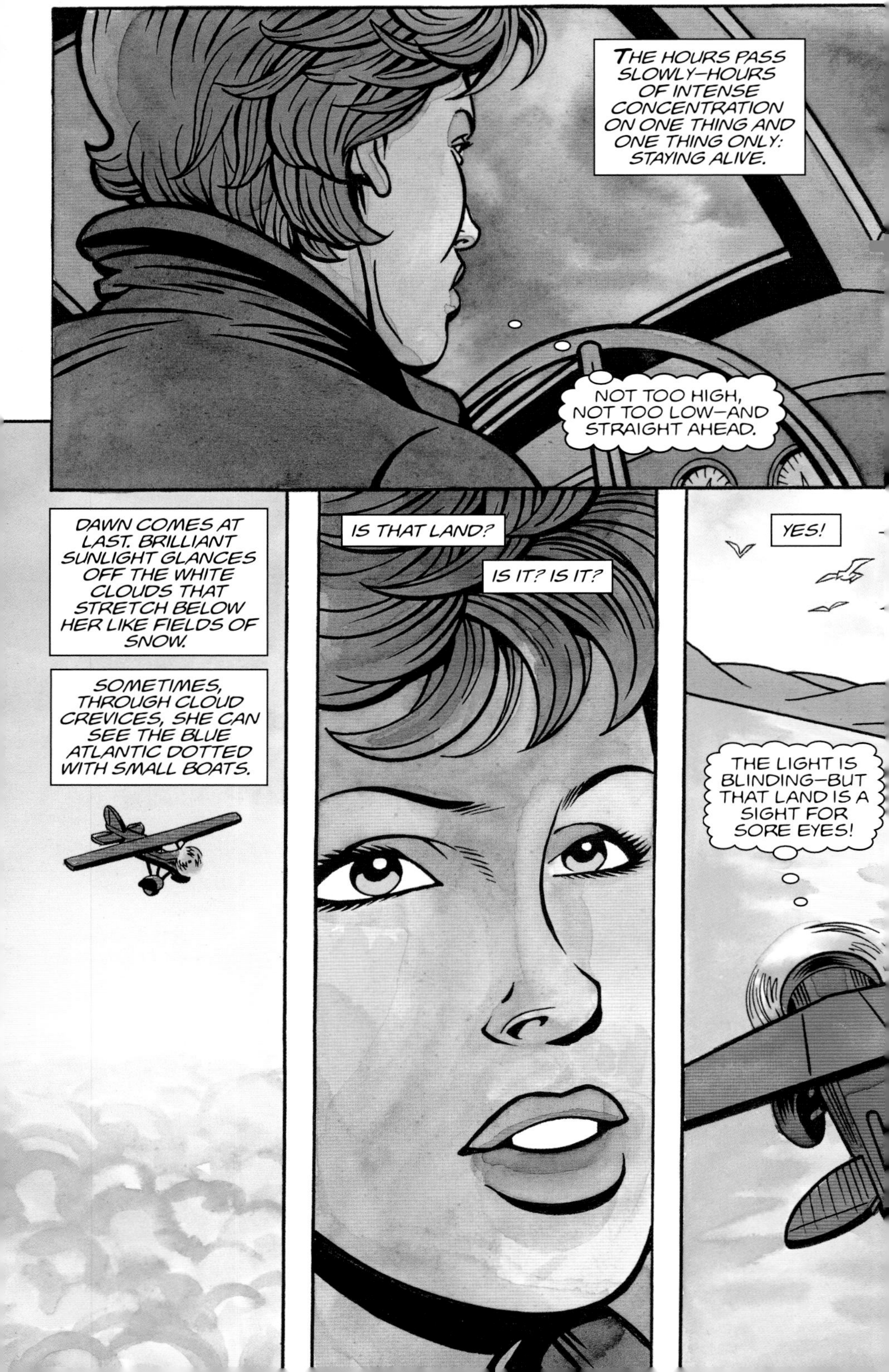
THE HOURS PASS SLOWLY—HOURS OF INTENSE CONCENTRATION ON ONE THING AND ONE THING ONLY: STAYING ALIVE.
NOT TOO HIGH, NOT TOO LOW—AND STRAIGHT AHEAD.
DAWN COMES AT LAST. BRILLIANT SUNLIGHT GLANCES OFF THE WHITE CLOUDS THAT STRETCH BELOW HER LIKE FIELDS OF SNOW.
SOMETIMES, THROUGH CLOUD CREVICES, SHE CAN SEE THE BLUE ATLANTIC DOTTED WITH SMALL BOATS.
IS THAT LAND?
IS IT? IS IT?
YES!
THE LIGHT IS BLINDING—BUT THAT LAND IS A SIGHT FOR SORE EYES!

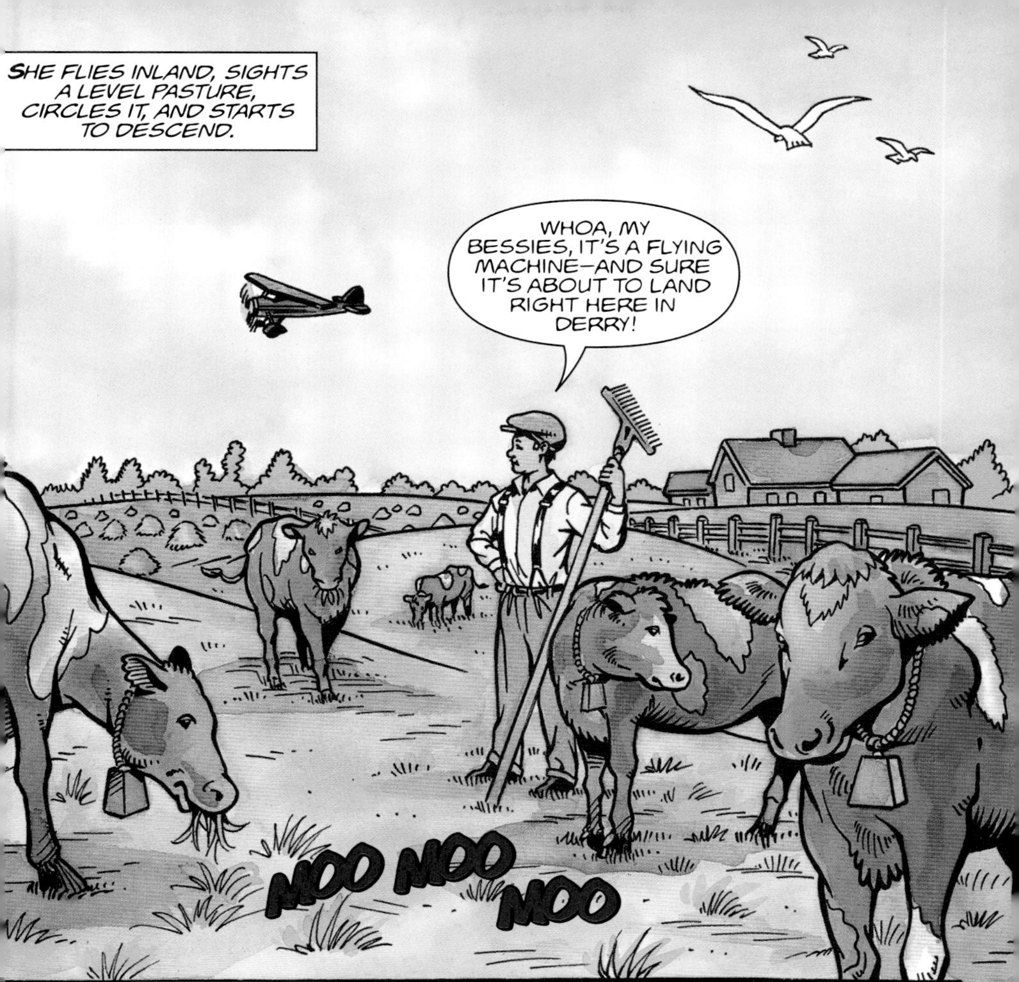
SHE FLIES INLAND, SIGHTS A LEVEL PASTURE, CIRCLES IT, AND STARTS TO DESCEND.
WHOA, MY BESSIES, IT'S A FLYING MACHINE—AND SURE IT'S ABOUT TO LAND RIGHT HERE IN DERRY!
MOO MOO MOO
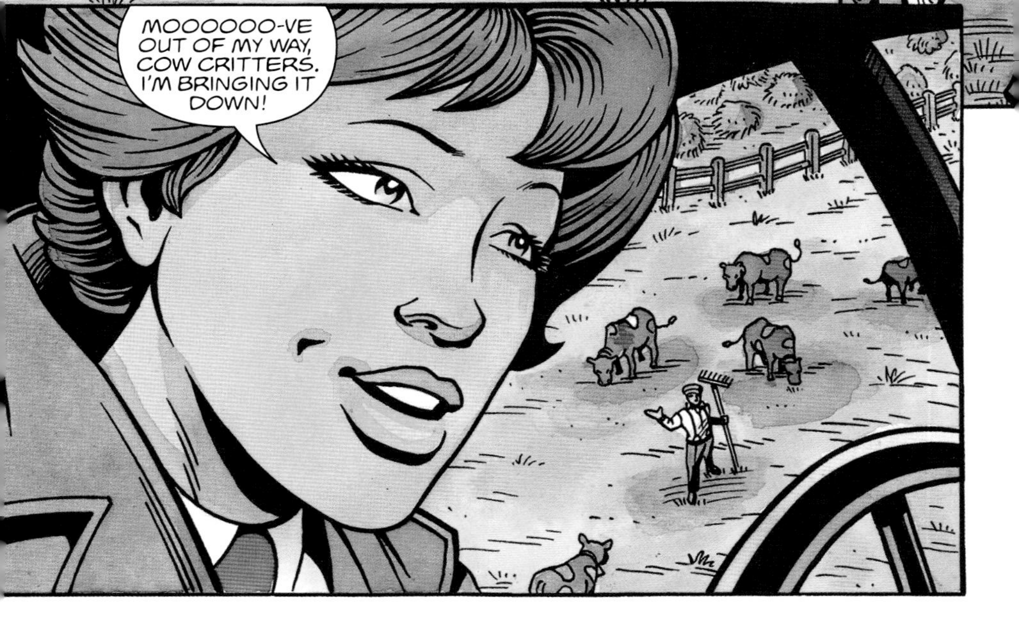
MOOOOOO-VE OUT OF MY WAY, COW CRITTERS. I'M BRINGING IT DOWN!

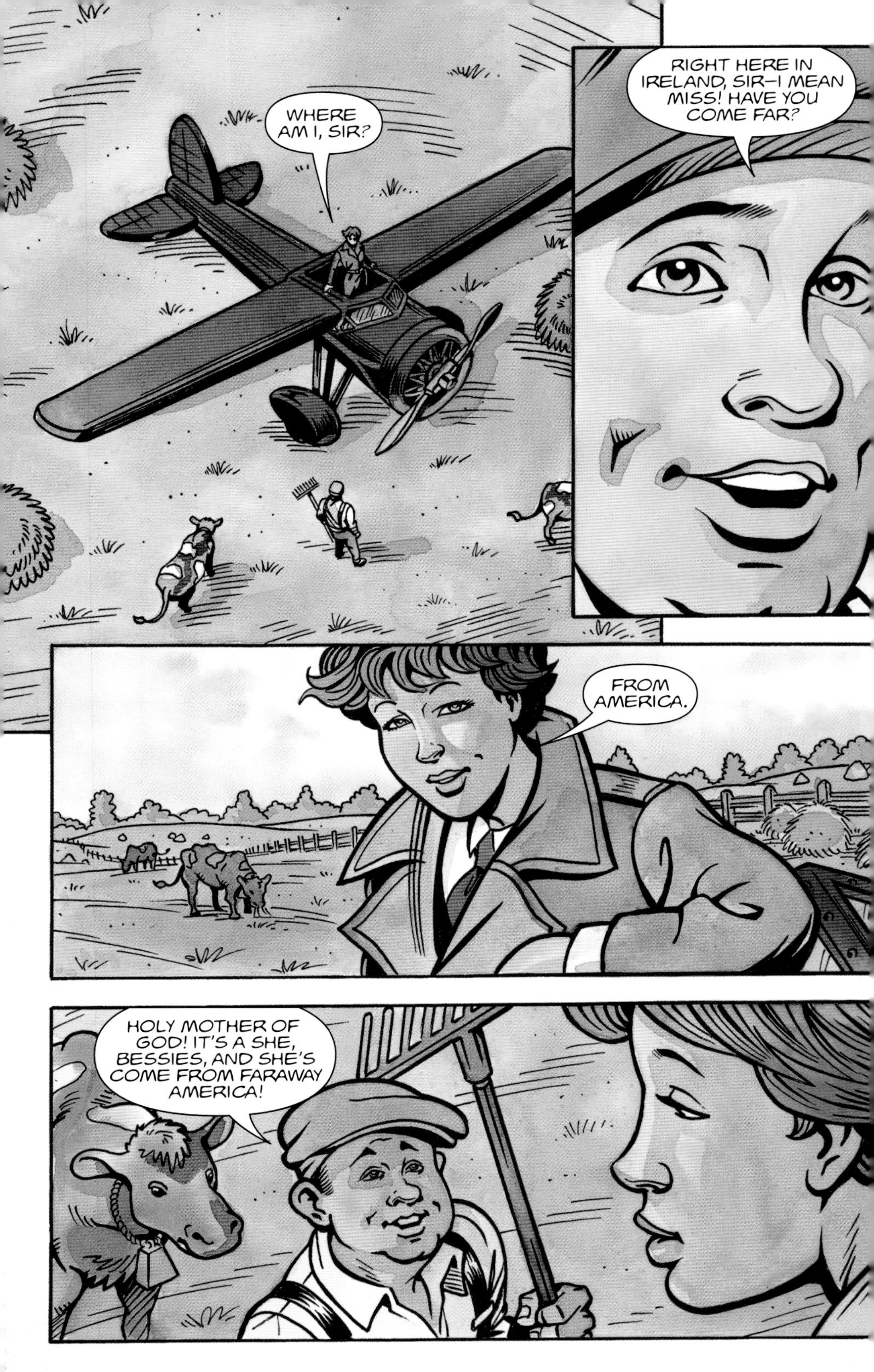
WHERE AM I, SIR?
RIGHT HERE IN IRELAND, SIR—I MEAN MISS! HAVE YOU COME FAR?
FROM AMERICA.
HOLY MOTHER OF GOD! IT'S A SHE, BESSIES, AND SHE'S COME FROM FARAWAY AMERICA!

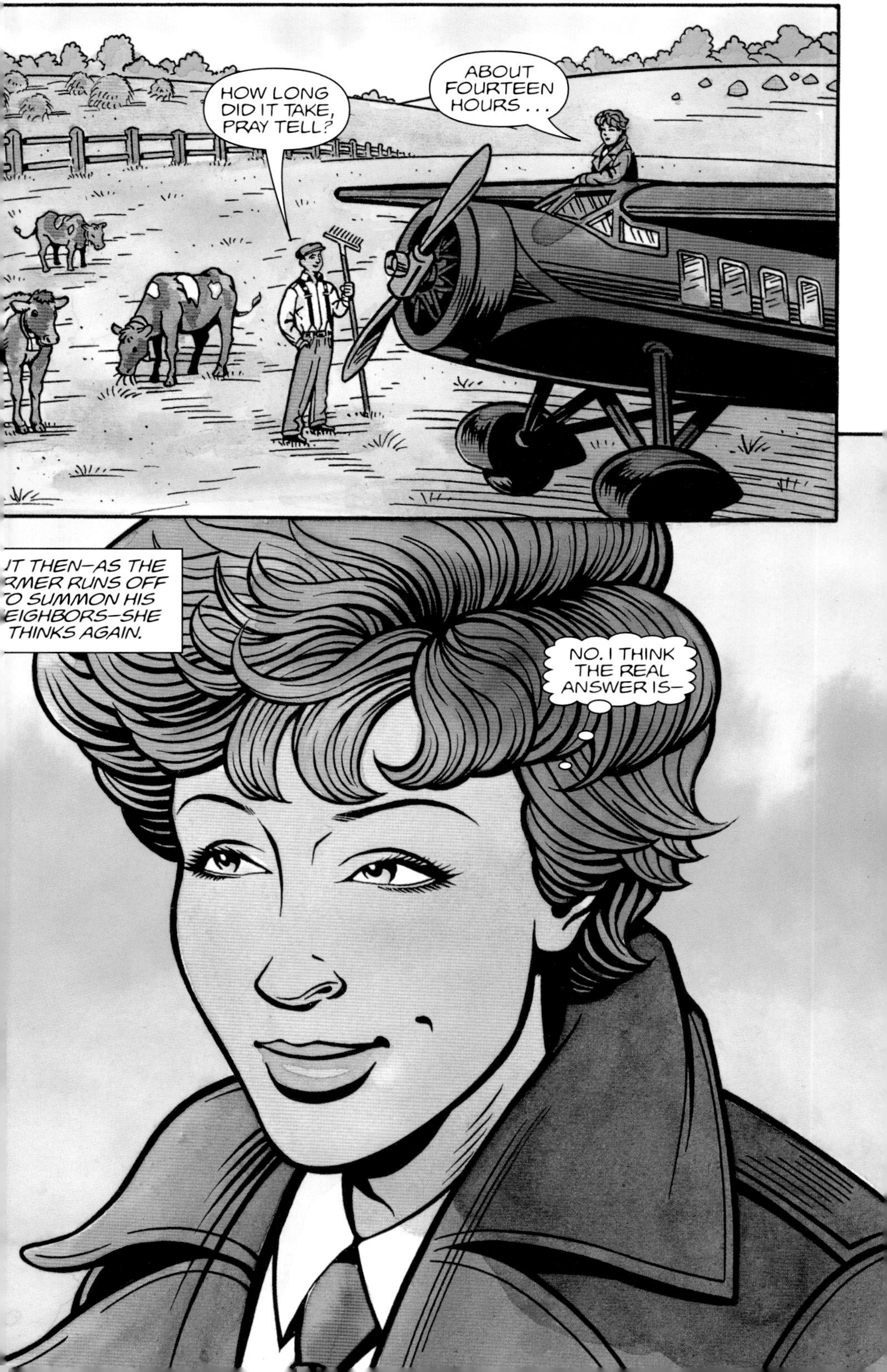
HOW LONG DID IT TAKE, PRAY TELL?
ABOUT FOURTEEN HOURS . . .
T THEN—AS THE RMER RUNS OFF O SUMMON HIS EIGHBORS—SHE THINKS AGAIN.
NO. I THINK THE REAL ANSWER IS—

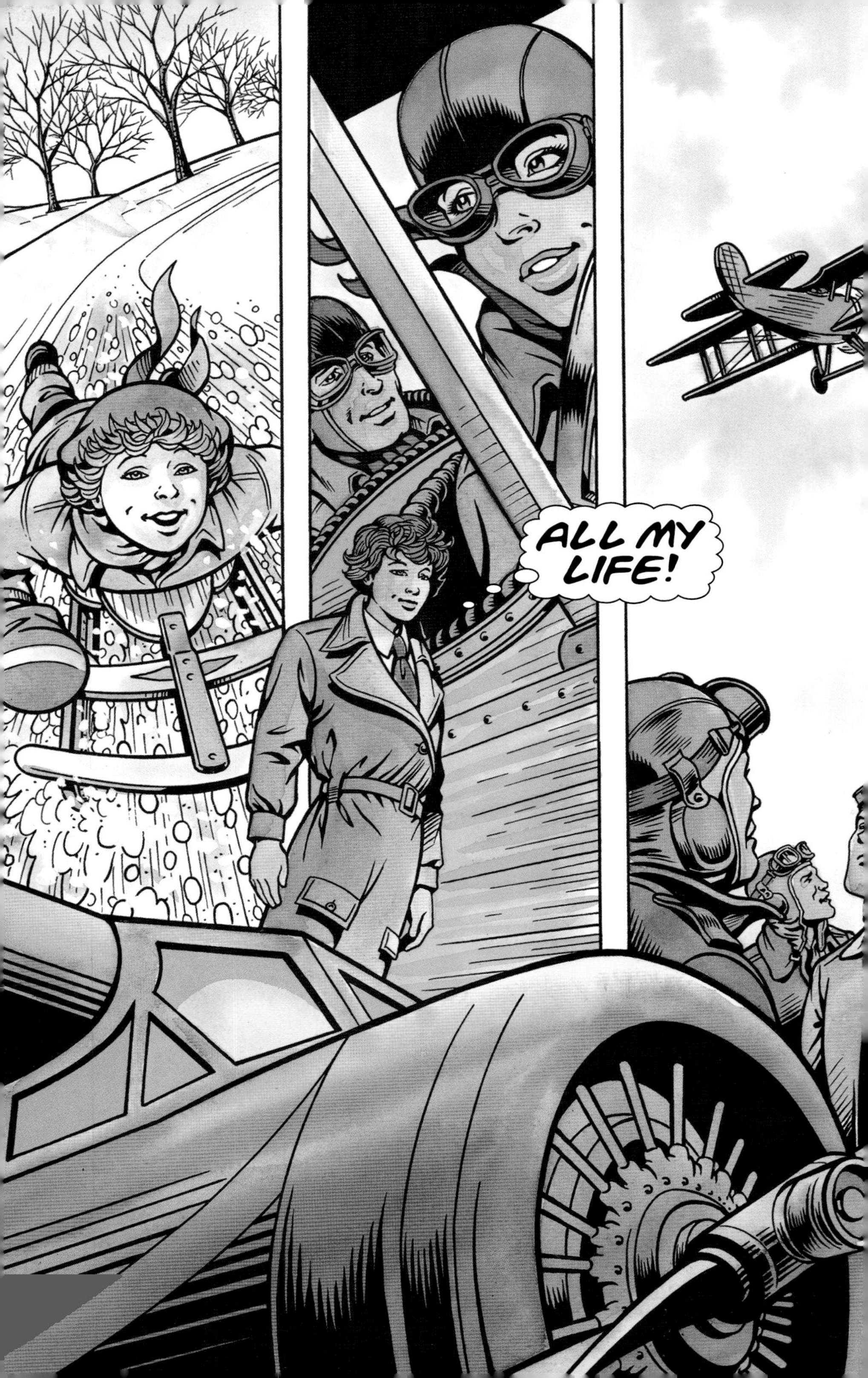
ALL MY LIFE!

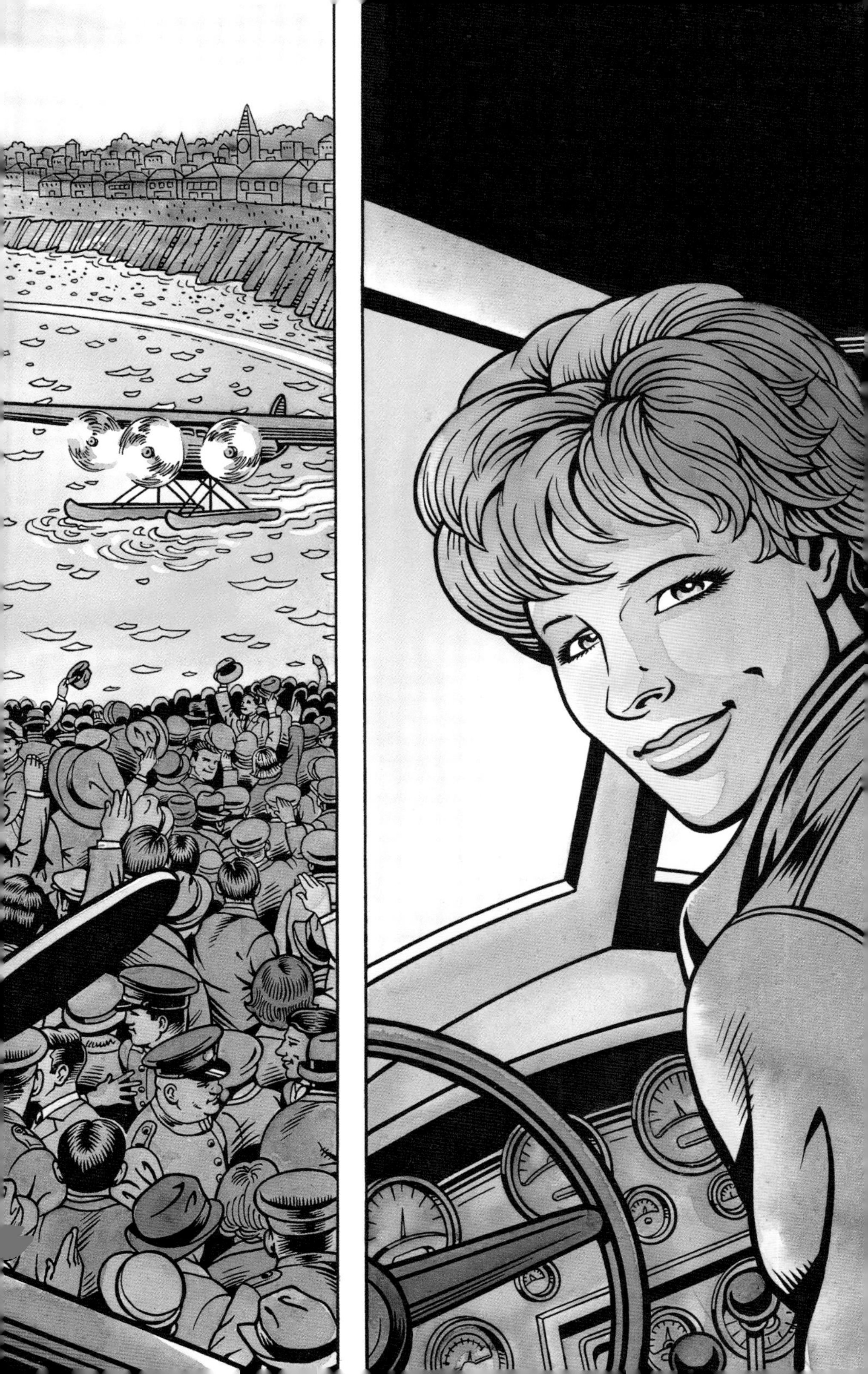

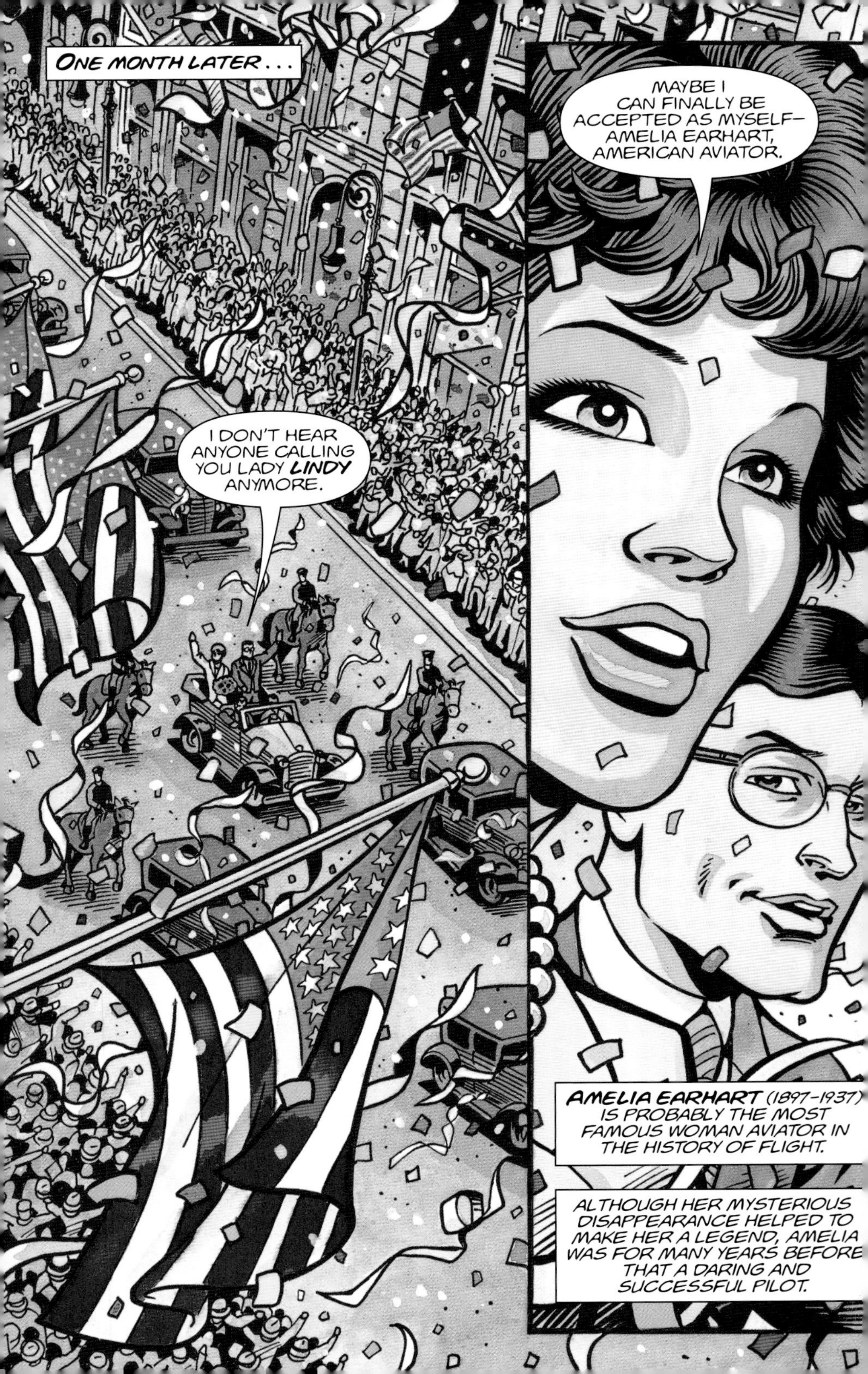
ONE MONTH LATER . . .
MAYBE I CAN FINALLY BE ACCEPTED AS MYSELF— AMELIA EARHART, AMERICAN AVIATOR.
I DON'T HEAR ANYONE CALLING YOU LADY LINDY ANYMORE.
AMELIA EARHART (1897–1937) IS PROBABLY THE MOST FAMOUS WOMAN AVIATOR IN THE HISTORY OF FLIGHT.
ALTHOUGH HER MYSTERIOUS DISAPPEARANCE HELPED TO MAKE HER A LEGEND, AMELIA WAS FOR MANY YEARS BEFORE THAT A DARING AND SUCCESSFUL PILOT.

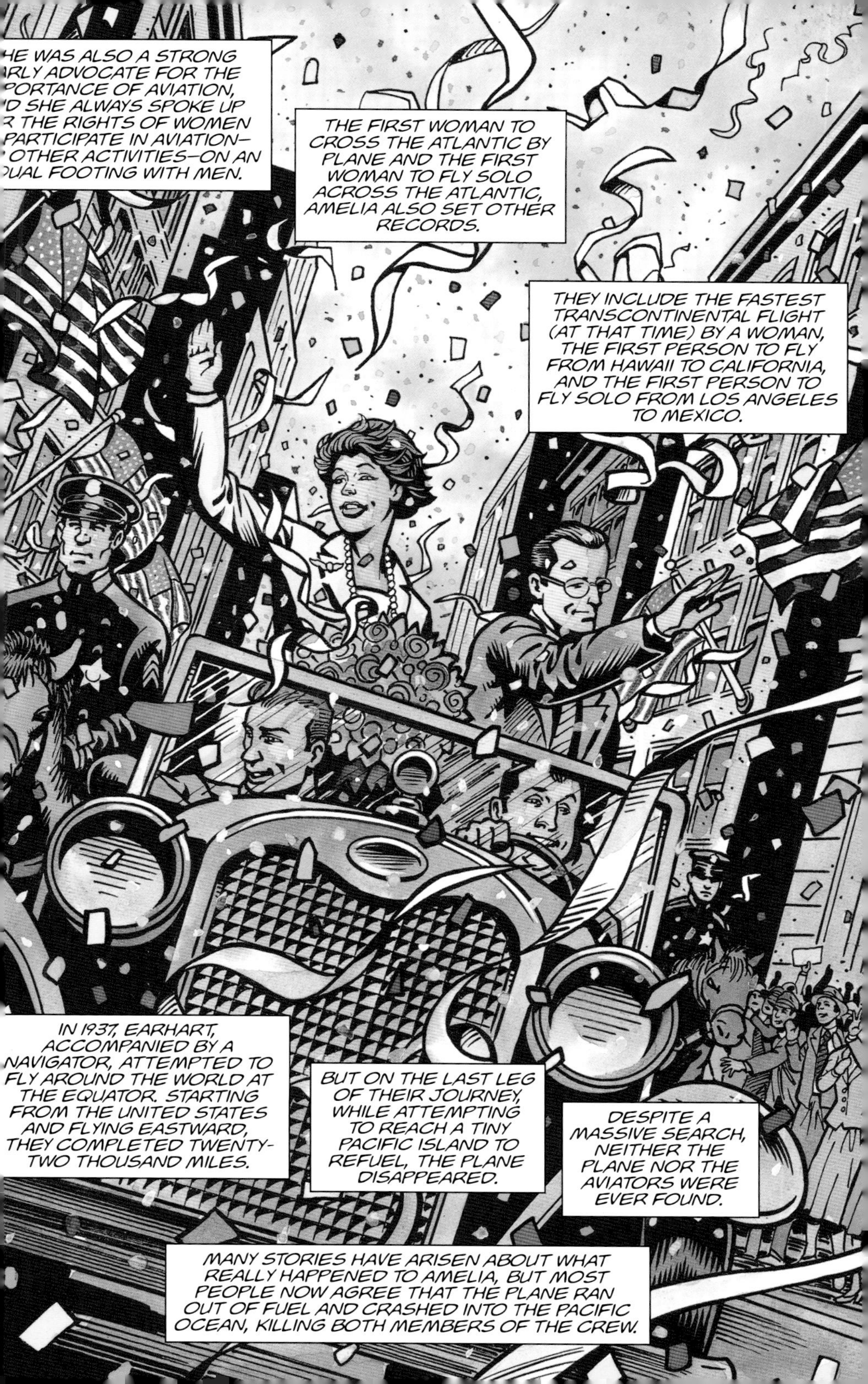
HE WAS ALSO A STRONG
RLY ADVOCATE FOR THE
PORTANCE OF AVIATION,
D SHE ALWAYS SPOKE UP
R THE RIGHTS OF WOMEN
PARTICIPATE IN AVIATION—
OTHER ACTIVITIES—ON AN
QUAL FOOTING WITH MEN.
THE FIRST WOMAN TO CROSS THE ATLANTIC BY PLANE AND THE FIRST WOMAN TO FLY SOLO ACROSS THE ATLANTIC, AMELIA ALSO SET OTHER RECORDS.
THEY INCLUDE THE FASTEST TRANSCONTINENTAL FLIGHT (AT THAT TIME) BY A WOMAN, THE FIRST PERSON TO FLY FROM HAWAII TO CALIFORNIA, AND THE FIRST PERSON TO FLY SOLO FROM LOS ANGELES TO MEXICO.
IN 1937, EARHART, ACCOMPANIED BY A NAVIGATOR, ATTEMPTED TO FLY AROUND THE WORLD AT THE EQUATOR. STARTING FROM THE UNITED STATES AND FLYING EASTWARD, THEY COMPLETED TWENTY-TWO THOUSAND MILES.
BUT ON THE LAST LEG OF THEIR JOURNEY, WHILE ATTEMPTING TO REACH A TINY PACIFIC ISLAND TO REFUEL, THE PLANE DISAPPEARED.
DESPITE A MASSIVE SEARCH, NEITHER THE PLANE NOR THE AVIATORS WERE EVER FOUND.
MANY STORIES HAVE ARISEN ABOUT WHAT REALLY HAPPENED TO AMELIA, BUT MOST PEOPLE NOW AGREE THAT THE PLANE RAN OUT OF FUEL AND CRASHED INTO THE PACIFIC OCEAN, KILLING BOTH MEMBERS OF THE CREW.

ROBERT BURLEIGH HAS WRITTEN MANY BOOKS FOR CHILDREN INCLUDING *INTO THE AIR: THE STORY OF THE WRIGHT BROTHERS FIRST FLIGHT,* ALSO ILLUSTRATED BY BILL WYLIE, AND *HOOPS,* ILLUSTRATED BY STEPHEN T. JOHNSON, A *BOOKLIST* EDITORS' CHOICE AND A *SCHOOL LIBRARY JOURNAL* BEST BOOK OF THE YEAR. MR. BURLEIGH LIVES WITH HIS WIFE IN CHICAGO, ILLINOIS.

BILL WYLIE HAS ILLUSTRATED MANY COMIC BOOKS, INCLUDING THE SECRET DEFENDERS SERIES AND SINGLE ISSUES OF THE SERIES NOMAD, NIGHTSTALKERS, AND NAMOR. HIS FIRST GRAPHIC NOVEL WAS *INTO THE AIR: THE STORY OF THE WRIGHT BROTHERS FIRST FLIGHT,* ALSO WRITTEN BY ROBERT BURLEIGH, WHICH *SCHOOL LIBRARY JOURNAL* PRAISED FOR BEING A "WINNING COMBINATION" OF "HIGH-INTEREST FORMAT AND HIGH-INTEREST STORY." MR. WYLIE LIVES WITH HIS WIFE IN BROOKLYN, NEW YORK.